(THE JANUS GATE)

FUTURE IMPERFECT

STAR TREK®
THE ORIGINAL SERIES

book two of three

THE JANUS GATE

FUTURE IMPERFECT

L. A. Graf

Based upon STAR TREK®
created by Gene Roddenberry

POCKET BOOKS
New York   London   Toronto   Sydney   Singapore

An *Original* Publication of POCKET BOOKS

POCKET BOOKS, a division of Simon & Schuster, Inc.
1230 Avenue of the Americas, New York, NY 10020

STAR TREK is a Registered Trademark of Paramount Pictures.

This book is published by Pocket Books, a division of Simon & Schuster, Inc., under exclusive license from Paramount Pictures.

ISBN: 0-671-03636-X

First Pocket Books printing June 2002

10 9 8 7 6 5 4 3 2 1

POCKET and colophon are registered trademarks of Simon & Schuster, Inc.

For information regarding special discounts for bulk purchases, please contact Simon & Schuster Special Sales at 1-800-456-6798 or business@simonandschuster.com

Printed in the U.S.A.

THE JANUS GATE

FUTURE IMPERFECT

Chapter One

THE CARGO SHUTTLE BUCKED and shuddered, caught in a savage wind gust that had erupted out of a still, clear dawn. Sulu threw a disbelieving look out his cockpit window at Tlaoli's garnet-dusted sky and saw nothing in its sunlit haze to indicate a storm brewing. He could even see plumes of mist, the exhaled breath of hidden caves, rising straight and calm from the splintered landscape of karst and sinkholes below him. But despite the testimony of his eyes, his hands and ears told him that a relentless avalanche of air had the shuttle clenched in its grip. Sulu could feel the little ship falling farther and farther away from the stable, banking turn he'd begun just a moment ago.

He'd been exultantly heading for home then, after locating a shadowy figure moving through the wilderness of fractured rock, a figure that could only be his own lost captain. That unexpected success, made on the one brief reconnaissance flight Sulu had been allowed before evacuating the rest of the stranded landing party from Tlaoli, had buoyed his spirits amazingly. After hours aboard the *Enterprise* fighting Tlaoli's unpredictable gravitational shifts and dangerous power drains, while Captain Kirk and his rescue party struggled to survive the killing cold and darkness of the caverns where the original landing party had been lost, it seemed as if the strange alien force that guarded this ancient planet had finally lost its grasp on them.

Then from nowhere, gale-force winds roared out of a clear morning sky and sent the shuttle *Drake* skidding out of control.

Sulu gave up trying to fight the wind's pull and instead swung the shuttle hard into it, hoping he could break through to calmer air on the other side. But before the roar of the engines had time to deepen in response, before the straining nacelles could even start to shriek in protest, the *Drake* snapped to a stop and hung frozen in midair. Sulu's breath caught in his throat. In all his years of flying, in craft as small as hang gliders and as large as the *Enterprise,* he had never before felt this kind of sudden arrest. This wasn't one of the alien planet's odd gravitational perturbations, or the unstoppable power drain that had made the *Enterprise* nearly crash into its surface only a few hours ago. This was simply—stillness.

Sulu had no idea how long it lasted—a few microseconds? half a minute?—but there was absolutely no doubt about how it ended. The *Drake* was slammed out of its stillness by the unmistakable blow of an atmospheric shock wave. Sulu's inner ears told him the little ship was flipping sideways, but the sudden darkness outside his cockpit window blocked any view of what had exploded down on the planet, or which way he was being thrown by the blast. The deafening noise of detonation caught up with him an instant later, fast enough and loud enough to tell Sulu he'd been near the epicenter of whatever had just blown up.

The only thing that saved him from losing control entirely was the adrenaline spiking in his blood from the wind gusts he'd been fighting a moment before. Sulu found himself responding almost before he was consciously aware of the need to do so, flinging the shuttle across the vector of the blast instead of fighting it, then spiraling its uncontrolled tumble into a gravity-assisted dive that made the metal nacelles scream in protest as he exceeded their strain limit. That sound sharpened into a howl of torn metal as Sulu hauled the *Drake* up out of its dive, praying every second that the blinding smoke around him wouldn't suddenly turn into rocky ground. When he finally got control of the *Drake* again, it was riding the bow wave of the explosion like an awkward surfer. The shuttle's steep, nose-up position told Sulu more clearly than the red-flashing lights on his controls that he'd done some permanent damage to the nacelles. But for now, he was content to hold the *Drake* in whatever position gave it some aerodynamic equilibrium, letting the wave of battered air sweep him ever farther from the epicenter of the explosion.

The smoke began to clear away from his cockpit windows, revealing tantalizing shreds and scraps of ruddy light through its breaks. It didn't look much like the cold rose-quartz dawn Sulu had taken the shuttle up into. In fact, if he didn't know better, he would swear the light had the sullen humid glare of the tropics. Sulu glanced down at his instrument panel, whose gauges still flashed overloads and error readings from the strange subspace interference fields that had made them all useless on Tlaoli. With a sudden and completely unjustified intuition, he swept a hand across the bank of power switches, zeroing them all to black, then watching them as they booted back up again. Each and every gauge came back a steady, reliable green, even the one warning him about the high levels of tension where the shuttle's hull met its damaged nacelles. The subspace interference had vanished.

Wherever he was now, Sulu thought, it was nowhere near the strange alien caves of Tlaoli.

The smoke thinned a little, then, without warning, the shuttle surged away from the spreading wake of the explosion and into clear air as the propulsion of its own engines finally outpaced the weakening atmospheric shock wave it had been swept up in. Sulu saw a looming shadow of hills ahead of him and pulled the *Drake* up as gently as he dared, trying to spare its weakened nacelles now that he was free of the blast wave. He was so intent on crafting a low-stress, minimum-clearance arc over those hills that it took him a long moment to realize they were completely the wrong color.

The one thing the *Enterprise* had known about Tlaoli before it sent survey teams down to study it was that the little planet was ancient and dry and mostly barren of life. The only vegetation Sulu had seen, in his three trips down to the alien planet, consisted of drought-gnarled trees and thorny shrubs the same dry gray-brown as the rocks and dirt around them. But *these* hills looked as if they were made of sodden emerald velvet. Their canopied trees rose in such a lush tangle that Sulu couldn't see any trace of bare ground between them. In fact, the only things that didn't glow a vivid shade of green were the violet-gray strands of mist and ground-fog nestled in the hollows and winding valleys of the forested hills.

Sulu pursed his lips to whistle in amazement, but to his surprise, he found them too dry to allow any noise to come out. That observation led to another—his hands were shaking despite their tight grip on the *Drake*'s helm control, and his pulse was pounding so strongly that he could actually feel it throb beneath the skin of one temple. He would have put the fear down to the aftermath of being engulfed by a mysterious explosion if he hadn't caught his gaze straying again and again to a gauge that he normally paid no attention to. With a start, Sulu focused on it now—and realized that the fundamental constant of planetary gravity to which all of his other shuttle instruments calibrated themselves had shifted up by three percent. The reading confirmed what some subconscious part of Sulu's brain must have already noticed and understood and been horrified by.

The *planet* he was on now was *not* Tlaoli.

Sulu gritted his teeth, fighting the urge to bank the *Drake* around at the speed he'd normally have used in an emergency, as if he could somehow find his way back to Tlaoli and the *Enterprise* just by reversing course. Some rational part of his brain knew that all the maneuver would accomplish would be to finish the job of tearing off the cargo shuttle's nacelles and strand him on this unknown world forever. But it still seemed worthwhile to find out what had exploded upon his arrival here—a wormhole? an antimatter/matter space warp?—so he maneuvered the wounded shuttle into a slow, gentle arc and watched the crushed-velvet hills drift below him.

The verdant palette of chlorophyll-based colors should have warned Sulu that this unknown planet probably wasn't anywhere near as empty of animal life as Tlaoli had been. But it still came as a shock to him when the green mass of forest abruptly ended, towering a surprising height above the black rock walls that succeeded it. Sulu's startled gaze followed those walls up toward the horizon and saw them merge with others, rise in height, then become blunt terraces bristling with spikes—no, not spikes, he realized as the *Drake* came closer, but hollow pipes, pipes that were moving sideways, pointing outward, turning to aim—at him!

Sulu cursed and wrenched the *Drake* into an evasive maneuver, momentarily forgetting the shuttle's torn nacelles. Fortunately, his downward dive kept torque to a minimum, at least until he was forced to pull up out of it. In the meantime, he watched puffs of what looked like smoke emerge from the snouts of the moving weapons and wondered just how primitive this unknown culture was. Clearly, they recognized even a distant flying object as a threat and were prepared to shoot at it...but what exactly were they shooting? Nothing seemed to explode near him or on the ground below, even long after the smoke had emerged, so it wasn't some kind of explosive device or torpedo. Projectiles, perhaps, small enough to make no sign when they missed their mark and fell to the ground.

The weapons along the black stone terraces slowly tracked him as Sulu hurtled down toward them, coaxing the shuttle out of its dive by painful fractions of arc, wincing as he heard the occasional shriek of metal ripping just a little further. He could tell that the barrels of the weapons weren't able to keep pace with his headlong dive, although to his surprise they all seemed to be trying. That was a gift he hadn't expected, that the crews who were manning those installations wouldn't realize that what came down must—if it were to survive—head back up again. If even one weapon stopped trying to track along his path and instead paused, waiting to meet him on the way back up again, Sulu was doomed.

But none of them did. He ground out the last nerve-racking curve that lifted the shuttle from descent to ascent again, then began a horizontal turn at an angle he hoped they wouldn't expect. It took him not back toward the rain-forested hills he had come from, but directly toward the cloud of smoke that still hung thick and sullen over the tallest towers of what now looked unmistakably like a fortress.

The shuttle darted into the smoke, and Sulu lost all sight of the weapons following him. He could still hear them, though, a constant pounding thunder that made his head ache and his eyes blink in conditioned response to the blows of sound. Still, nothing more than sound seemed to hit the *Drake* as it fled with excruciating slowness through the lingering remnants of the explosion that had greeted it upon arrival.

Sulu began an upward climb while he was still shrouded in smoke, grimacing as his evasive maneuver carried him so close to one black stone tower that he almost thought he could see a glare of eyes through its narrow slitted windows. Then the smoke cleared again and he found himself high above the central hub of this kilometers-wide installation. The weapons around the fringes no longer seemed to be aiming or firing at him—no puffs of smoke drifted out of their long hollow barrels. By now, however, Sulu was feeling too battered by fate to take that for a good sign. He glanced around the hazy tropical sky, then finally remembered that his long-range scanners would work here and slapped a hand down to activate the vessel-detection screen. It took only one glance to tell him that his pessimistic instincts had been correct. A raft of small yellow lights lay directly astern, already matching the *Drake*'s not-very-impressive velocity. And even as he watched, the scanner showed a flicker around the nose of the foremost ship that indicated some kind of power field had been detected there.

Sulu groaned and straightened the *Drake* out to give its nacelles the most support he could, then jacked the engines up until the tensions measured along the hull flickered between yellow and red. To his surprise, the unseen chase ships only matched his increase in velocity—they didn't try to close the gap between them. Now why, if they could have gone that fast to begin with, Sulu wondered, had they waited for him to increase speed before they did? Was there some minimum firing range they needed for the energy weapons that his scanners showed being fired now from several ships? If so, perhaps they had miscalculated it for a ship as strange to them as his must be. Not a shiver or rattle went through the *Drake* as those power flickers winked on and off the scanner's detection screen.

He left the swath of central towers behind and crossed back over black stone terraces, empty of everything except the turning barrels of weapons that protruded from the edge like fangs. A towering green tsunami of forest appeared beyond the final perimeter wall, rising almost to the shuttle's altitude and promising safety if only he could disappear into its deepest hollows. But the same glance that told Sulu how close he was to shelter also showed him the turning spikes of the weapon barrels, swinging around in unison to intercept his course. He groaned in dismay and self-disgust. After all his years in Starfleet Academy and aboard Starfleet's premier deep-space vessel, he should have known better!

Sulu had made the most basic mistake of space exploration, assuming that the alien strategists who commanded in this fortress would follow the same rules of tactics as known civilizations did. Humans or Vulcans or Klingons never fired antispacecraft weapons if there were more of their own fighters than enemies aloft, because of the risk of being hit by friendly fire. But these fortress fighters were either a more ruthless or more self-sacrificing lot. Sulu began—much too late—to lift the *Drake* up to a less dangerous altitude, and saw the raft of yellow dots behind him on the long-range scanner increase altitude to match his without ever getting closer. That gap suddenly made sense to him. It would give the perimeter weapons a clear interval to fire before they encountered their own ships.

It also gave Sulu an idea.

Praying that the *Drake*'s abused nacelles would take the strain, he began to level the shuttle off at an altitude that still kept him dangerously close to the unknown weapons ahead. Just as he expected, the long-range scanners reported his chasers doing the same thing. Then, just as he crossed over the edge of the black stone terrace and into weapons range, Sulu began a sharp banking turn at the tightest angle he could manage and still keep the nacelles from shearing off. It took the *Drake* into the sudden thundering fire of the ground weapons, and this time Sulu could hear the sickening thuds as projectiles hit and cratered the shuttle's duranium hull without ever breaking through. He winced, but held his course. The *Drake* was a cargo shuttle, never meant for battle, and its shields were designed to ward off particles of space dust and fragments of comets, not armored projectiles. Sulu wasn't sure how many of those impacts it could take without breaking apart at the seams, but he was gambling that it wouldn't be long until the fusillade ceased.

He craned his head to watch the weapons from the side of his cockpit as he swung the shuttle around, and allowed himself a grim smile of satisfaction. These unknown fighters might not be predictable, but they were certainly consistent. Once again, all of the weapons were tracking him in unison, following the *Drake* faithfully around on its 180-degree turn, until they found themselves pointed at their own ships as well as at the intruder. There was a moment of confusion when waves of projectiles slammed into the leading chase ships, bringing several of them down with surprising efficiency before the thunder of the ground weapons rolled into silence and smoke drifted away from their empty barrels.

The phalanx of chase ships was in chaos now. Sulu took advantage of it to thread his way through them and cut sideways, slipping over a different part of the outer stone wall before the ground weapons got a chance to retrain their sights on him. He lifted the *Drake* with a stomach-churning lurch that just cleared the towering wall of green on the other side, then settled down to hug the tops of those monstrous tree canopies as he raced for the hills on the horizon.

It took the remaining chase ships a few moments to regroup, and another minute for Sulu's vessel-detection screen to give him the bad news he'd expected. Now that they were all past the edge of the installation, there was no doubt that those alien ships were faster than the *Drake*, probably faster than it had been even before the powerful explosion back at the towers had half-torn its nacelles off. He jacked the engines back up as high as he dared, but he could still set only a snail's pace compared with the ships behind him. It was only a few moments before they were in visual range again, a half-dozen blunt-nosed attack ships with darkened cockpit windows and parabolic wings. Sulu could see through the side of his cockpit the heat-wave shimmer of the energy weapons that the scanner insisted were being fired from their snouts. Still, the *Drake* flew on without so much as a lurch or twitch of response.

The cargo shuttle's strange imperviousness to their weapons must have been apparent to the attackers, too—one buzzed him overhead, close enough to make the *Drake* shudder and roll in the wake vortex trailing behind it. Sulu dragged the shuttle back to equilibrium with difficulty—the torn nacelles had a tendency to exaggerate every loss of stability into a sideways roll. It wasn't until a second attacker buzzed and flew off, leaving him enveloped in the heat-shimmer of its energy weapon's discharge, that Sulu noticed that all of his control panel gauges were black and powerless.

Sulu's eyebrows shot up as he realized what must be protecting the *Drake*. Chief Engineer Montgomery Scott had insisted on shielding the cargo shuttle's warp core and engines before Sulu took it down into the dangerous power-draining force fields of Tlaoli. Now the unknown aliens on this planet—maybe even the same ones who built that underground installation—were firing some kind of energy-dispersive weapons at him. Those weapons would probably already have sent any normal shuttle plummeting down to the surface in an unpowered swan dive. The *Drake*'s stubborn ability to fly seemed to be making the aliens both impatient and, Sulu suspected, somewhat nervous.

He took a deep breath and slowed the engines again, holding his course as he was buzzed several more times by the flickering shapes of the attackers. There didn't seem to be anything else they could do but fire those heat-shimmer pulses at him, but that didn't make Sulu feel safe. With half-torn nacelles and a pockmarked hull, Sulu didn't want to spend hours being jostled by them or, even worse, drive the aliens to desperate tactics like a suicide ramming. He was equally reluctant to put the shuttle down while they watched and circled overhead like vultures to mark the spot where he landed. What he needed was to convince them they didn't need to worry about him anymore, and for that he was going to have to use a fairly desperate tactic himself.

Sulu inched the *Drake* upward a few hundred meters to give himself a little maneuvering room and a better view of the landscape below. There was rain forest everywhere below him now. The alien fortress had dwindled to a distant smudge of smoke behind a range of hills, and ahead of him the sky was painted with tiger stripes of orange, saffron, and crimson around a setting tropical sun. The forest was vast and featureless, webbed everywhere with streamers of violet-tinted fog as the cooling air drizzled out its moisture. Then, off to one side, Sulu caught a glimpse of what looked like a shattered mirror whose tiger stripes matched the sky. He wasn't sure if it was a lake or an enormous river, but at least it was something to orient himself by in this endless span of green. Sulu took a deep breath, waited for one last attacker to shower him in heat-shimmer, then cut all power to the shuttle's engines.

They made them practice this maneuver in Starfleet simulators, over and over again, but Sulu discovered that it didn't really prepare you for the gut-wrenching feel of fading momentum and dragging gravity, the sidelong plunge that couldn't really be called a roll, the spinning plummet that increased with such shocking speed that by the time he cut the engines in again he was far closer to the forest canopy than he had planned.

The trees closed in around the shuttle while he was still trying to pull it out of its dive, and Sulu heard a rising shriek from the nacelles as their ripped seams tore open further. He made one last effort to lower his speed, but the torque was too much for the hull. With a sound almost like an explosion, one nacelle tore off completely, followed a moment later by the other. The *Drake* plunged downward, still spinning uncontrollably but powered enough to turn its deadly vertical plunge into a dangerous horizontal slide. And the trees themselves helped, their many branches flickering past too fast to see but braking his momentum just the same. The *Drake*'s shields warded off the worst impacts from the larger branches, although Sulu didn't think they would be much help if he hit one of the monstrous trunks that must rise through this greenery somewhere. But as the ship twisted and lurched and skidded slowly downward through the darkening shade of the canopy, the one thing he was sure of was that it must have looked to his pursuers like a real, honest-to-God crash.

He ended up sliding only slightly canted along a humus-littered forest floor, and finally bumping to an almost laughably gentle stop against a fallen log whose diameter matched the shuttle's height. Sulu cut the engines off again with shaking fingers and wondered if he should power-down the warp core in case its shielding had been damaged. He would think about that in a minute, he promised himself, after he caught his breath and wiped the sweat of suddenly humid air off his face. The shuttle's battered hull must have sprung a leak on its way down through the forest. He would know soon enough if there was anything toxic to humans in this planet's atmosphere.

In the meantime, he could finally relax long enough to realize that he was now a hunted man on an alien planet whose name he didn't know and whose location could be almost anywhere in the galaxy.

"Oh…this isn't good…." Shaking her head slowly, Yuki Smith did something Pavel Chekov had never dreamed a Starfleet security guard would do—she retreated several steps toward the center of the small karst plateau, as though contemplating running away entirely. "He's *crying!*" she whispered fiercely in Chekov's direction. "They don't train security guards to deal with crying."

Chekov didn't think it worth pointing out that Starfleet Academy didn't exactly offer electives in dealing with crying for Astrogation majors, either. Instead, he just nodded as though her objection made perfect sense, and kept his attention focused on the boy who knelt a few meters in front of them on the edge of the uneven plateau.

The boy wasn't really crying anymore. The tears had lasted only a few wrenching, naked moments, when Chekov and Smith had first cornered him at the edge of the steep drop-off. Now, the only remnant of the boy's tears was a sheen of wetness on his cheeks and a ragged edge to his breathing that made it sound as though he took three quick breaths on every too-deep inhalation. His fear had already began to mutate into something else—something cunning and more productive. Chekov couldn't precisely identify the emotion glowing in the boy's keen hazel stare, but he'd seen glimpses of it on the face of the adult James Kirk during the last eighteen hours. He suspected it meant that even a very young James Kirk would prove a formidable adversary.

"Listen to me." Chekov struggled to pitch his tone just the right distance between solicitude and belligerence to keep the boy from bristling. He was close enough to his own teen years to remember how much he hated adults speaking to him as though he were stupid, but just far enough away from them to appreciate how stupid teenaged boys often were. "We're not going to hurt you. You said your father is in Starfleet. Then you know we're here to protect civilians, not to hurt them."

The boy's eyes flicked back and forth between gold uniform and red, touching briefly on sleeves, insignia, and waists. Anticipating the boy's concern, Chekov spread his arms out to either side. "Look—we don't even have weapons."

It seemed to bother the boy a little that this stranger would understand what he was thinking. Sinking back on his heels, he thrust his chin vaguely in Chekov's direction. "What's that?"

It took Chekov a moment to realize he meant the small device still curled in Chekov's left hand. "A compass. For finding our bearings." He held his hand out flat in front of him so the boy could see the imprinted face and the swinging, hair-fine needle. Moving his hand slightly in a more distinct offering, he said, "Here. Take it."

Interest moved across the boy's face, replacing suspicion for the first time since they'd pinned him here. Once again, Chekov was reminded of Kirk's fearless curiosity, and he felt an irrational surge of guilt to be standing on the surface of an alien planet trying to reassure a fifteen-year-old version of his own commander. *Whatever this place did to you,* he found himself promising silently, *we'll fix it.* Because the thought of the *Enterprise* without Kirk in command was simply intolerable.

Stooping slowly, Chekov folded the compass closed and set it on the wind-polished rock at his feet. A nudge with his toe sent it skittering just far enough for the boy to lean forward and pick it up. Chekov watched him open it and turn it this way and that to check the needle's lazy swing, and tried to decide if the boy looked any calmer. Light from the freshly risen sun cut sharply across the boy's left shoulder, hiding half his expression in shadow as he bent over the small device. At least his breathing had steadied to a more regular rise and fall.

"We have a base camp about an hour's walk from here—" Chekov began.

This younger Kirk cut him off with the same impatient brusqueness that would strike fear into the hearts of his subordinates when he was twenty years more refined. "I saw it."

Chekov had to bite back an abashed and automatic, "Yes, sir." Instead, he fought to keep his voice rigorously even. "You should come back to camp with us—"

"No!" No longer some dim reflection of a great starship commander, he was just a boy again, obviously angered by the fear that flew too easily into his protest. His hand closed convulsively around the compass, and he glanced once, briefly, over his shoulder as though considering anew whether he could jump the deep rift between the karst towers. The sun made him squint and look back too quickly.

Chekov nodded, pretending not to notice the boy's vehemence. "Well, we can't stay out here all day."

"You can't, maybe." The boy lifted his chin in a brave defiance that wasn't at all feigned. "I'm not going anywhere."

You have no idea how true that is. If they didn't find out what this planet had done to Kirk—not to mention to Lieutenant Sulu, and possibly to Chekov himself—Chekov had a feeling none of them would be going anywhere anytime soon.

"Do you rank her?" The boy asked it suddenly, as though the thought had only just occurred to him.

Chekov glanced aside at Smith, strangely unsure how to respond even though the answer was obvious. He was too used to being the most junior member in any gathering to think of himself as ranking anyone. "Yes. I'm an officer." It was the first time he'd ever said that about himself.

"Then make her leave." The boy clicked the compass shut and folded it into his fist like a talisman. Alert hazel eyes locked on Smith, daring her to move. "She's security," he continued defiantly to Chekov. "You're just some command maven. If anybody can hurt me, it's her." He glanced away from her only long enough to pin Chekov with his stare. "Make her leave."

From ranking Starfleet officer to command maven in just under thirty seconds. A new galactic record, certainly. Still, the boy wasn't wrong, and Chekov had to give him credit for thinking clearly even if he was less than subtle about how he expressed it.

"Go on." He turned pointedly away from the boy, letting Kirk see that he was willing to turn his back while nodding to Smith. "Find Tomlinson and Martine. Tell them everything is all right."

He would have been disappointed if Smith hadn't hesitated at least a little. She glanced unhappily at the boy, then back at Chekov before finally answering his command with a businesslike "Aye, sir," and turning to climb back down the karst summit the way they'd first come up. She disappeared over the edge with an athletic vault that was much more graceful than Chekov suspected he himself would have managed.

"Who are Tomlinson and Martine?"

Chekov turned back to the boy, trying to exude the same easy confidence he had seen in a much older Kirk not so very long ago. "Two of the other officers stranded planetside with us. I don't want them to worry when they see I'm not with Smith."

Something about that made the boy frown slightly and lower his chin. "You're stranded here?" Morning shadows darkened his eyes again.

Chekov nodded. "There are twelve of us. About half are from the planetary survey team we came down here to rescue."

The boy gave a snort and a surprisingly mature, ironic smile. "Some rescue."

Chekov couldn't argue with him about that.

"So...where are we, exactly?"

"Tlaoli 4." A look that might have been fear flashed through the boy's eyes, so quickly masked that Chekov would have missed it if he'd glanced away. "A planet in sector alpha nineteen," he explained, still trying to decipher the boy's expression. A thought occurred to him, and he asked, "Where were you...before you were here?"

"On vacation. With my family in the Pantazis sector." He fought with himself a moment before admitting, "I don't know how I got here."

"We don't know how you got here, either." That

was likely to be the understatement of the day. "Did you... find yourself inside the cave?"

The boy straightened, obviously startled by the question. "Yeah."

"How did you find your way out in the dark?"

He shrugged. "It wasn't that dark. I mean, it was nighttime where I was before, so my eyes were already adjusted. The light from the stalactites or stalagmites or whatever was bright enough that I could see the hole in the roof."

Chekov remembered groping for his helmet in the thick darkness, stumbling into a sit, waiting with his heart in his throat while the cave around him whispered under its patina of frost. "There was no light in that cavern." He had never been more certain of anything in his life.

"There was just the one pillar. Gold light, like a transporter beam, only it never came together." The boy shrugged again, settling more comfortably back on his heels. "It was bright enough."

There was no light. He was sure of it—more sure than he was about anything else that had happened so far on Tlaoli—and the boy's equal certainty frightened him a little. But before he could ask for more detail about the claim, Kirk announced bluntly, "Now I get to ask a question."

Chekov nodded. "All right."

"What ship did you come in on? A starship?"

He nodded again, but hesitated before saying, "The *U.S.S. Enterprise.*" They had to breach the subject at some point, and sooner was no doubt better than later. Still, he found himself wishing Lieutenant Uhura were here, with her calm demeanor and expert communications skills.

To his surprise, the boy lit up at the mention of the ship's name. "Hey! I know your captain!"

Chekov felt a leaden weight fall into his stomach. "You do?"

"Robert April. He's a friend of my dad's. He came to our house for Christmas last year." Relief was palpable in the boy's smile as he climbed to his feet. He seemed even younger than before, the weight of his own safety suddenly cast off his shoulders and into adult hands that he trusted and loved. Chekov doubted he would ever again see James Kirk so vulnerable and acquiescent. "We can go talk to him. He knows where my dad is stationed—he'll know what to do."

Suddenly sorry he'd allowed the subject to arise, Chekov said carefully, "Captain April isn't here. In fact..." There was nothing to do now but plough headlong into it. "Robert April isn't captain of the *Enterprise* anymore."

"But I don't understand..." The boy frowned, knuckles white around the compass in his young hands as though clinging to that small device would make what he was about to hear less disturbing. "If Robert April's not captain of the *Enterprise*...who is?"

Chapter Two

TORN BETWEEN dismay and disbelief, Uhura stared across the flickering shadows of the Tlaoli caverns at the man who'd somehow been exchanged for their vanished shuttle pilot by the same mysterious alien force that had also swept away Captain Kirk and young Ensign Chekov. Could she really trust this older version of Sulu who claimed he'd been a starship captain once, who said that in his future both McCoy and Uhura were dead, and who insisted he'd never heard of Captain Kirk? Did she *really* know him the way her heart said she did, just because he looked and sounded and acted like the friend she had ordered to fly into danger a few hours ago?

"I'm sorry," the older Sulu said, scanning their faces in the uncertain light cast by Uhura and

McCoy's carbide lights. His deep voice held a note that hadn't been there before, one so unexpected that it took Uhura a moment to identify it as compassion. "I can see it upsets you, but it's true. In all my time in the service, there was never a Starfleet captain named Kirk, on the *Enterprise* or any other ship."

"But there should have been." It was an unreasoning protest when Uhura said it, but as she heard her own words echo back to her from the walls and healing chambers of this alien cavern, their implications sank in. "There should have been. And maybe there *would* have been, if we hadn't come here to Tlaoli." She turned to glance at McCoy and Sanner. "We thought this was an alien transporter, but what if it's actually a *time* transporter? If it moved Captain Kirk in such a way that he disappeared from our timeline before he became a captain—"

"Then *we* wouldn't remember him, either," Sanner objected.

McCoy grunted. "Maybe this machine is moving people between parallel dimensions where things are just a little different. Whenever we talk about the possibility of time travel, Spock always quotes some many-worlds hypothesis and says there's no such thing as a single timeline anyway."

"The Everett-Wheeler interpretation of quantum mechanics," the older Sulu said, nodding. "Of course, the Vulcans proved that was only partially right back in 2285, when they constructed the first artificial pinpoint singularity—" He broke off, looking rueful. "Um…Maybe I shouldn't be telling you that."

"If Doctor McCoy is right, it might not be our own future you're revealing," Uhura said. "But knowing about the future won't help us figure out what the transporter is doing. What we really need to compare is the past."

"To decide if we're from one shared timeline or two parallel dimensions?" Sulu began absently rolling up the right sleeve of his jacket, as if to get the blood-soaked and clammy fabric away from his skin, then saw what he was doing and pushed it down again. "Sorry about that. I don't suppose there's anything you can do about the temperature in here?"

"We could leave," McCoy suggested.

Uhura opened her mouth to agree with him, but Sanner forestalled her. "I'd like to take a look back down the conduit system before we do that, Lieutenant, to make sure we know just where that force field is sitting now." He saw Uhura's frown and tapped his unlit carbide lamp. "I promise I'll turn it off every couple of minutes to make sure I don't walk into any different time zones. But I've got an idea I want to check out."

"An idea about the development of the caves?"

"No, about the power supply for that alien transporter." Sanner thumbed the lever of his carbide and ignited the gas flame, then began poking through his backpack. "I made one of our spare carbide lamps into a portable stove while we were back at the base camp, just in case we found Lieutenant Sulu hurt and suffering from hypothermia. Now where the heck did it go?" He hauled out several coils of rope and bags of pitons before he excavated one of Scotty's carbide lamps, wearing what looked like an old-fashioned sunbonnet over the side that normally would have been open for illumination. "It's got lots of carbide rocks and water in it, so you can run it pretty hot, but you'll need to keep the heat contained. Maybe you can make a shelter out of the survey team's packs and those emergency blankets we were using before."

Uhura took the primitive heater from him, her frown deepening as she watched him stuff the rest of his gear back into his pack. "Zap, did you *plan* on doing more exploring while we were down here?"

The cave specialist gave her a look that was only half-abashed. "I didn't plan, exactly, I just thought if there was a chance to look around a little more...But I swear, Lieutenant, I'm not going caving now. If this power supply idea I've got checks out, we might actually get a handle on how this alien transporter works." He swung around before she could reply, apparently taking her permission for granted. "Lieutenant—uh, I mean, Captain Sulu? Could you tell me where the planet you came from is located?"

Some of his former suspicion crept back into Sulu's slitted eyes. "Why do you need to know?"

"I don't need an exact location, sir," Sanner said hastily. Apparently Uhura wasn't the only one who could feel the air of authority that proved this older version of Sulu really had been a starship captain. "I'm just trying to make a rough estimate of the transporter's power consumption."

Sulu considered that for a moment. "It's near the Omega Orionid cluster, close to the galactic fringe," he said at last. It wasn't a very specific location at all, encompassing many parsecs of space beyond the borders Uhura knew in her time, but it seemed enough to satisfy Sanner. The geologist made a note on the edge of the cave map he and Jaeger had reconstructed, then surprised Uhura with a chortle. "Better than I thought," he said cryptically, and went jingling off through the darkness toward the spiral passageway that led down to the rest of the alien conduit system.

"Our cave specialist," Uhura said to Sulu, hoping that would excuse the scientist's behavior.

"So I gathered." There was an amused note in the older man's voice that sounded familiar. After a moment, Uhura realized it was the way Captain Kirk sounded, too, when he was the one dealing with the dedicated single-mindedness of scientists. "Did you come to explore these caves because you knew there was an alien transporter device down here?"

"Not exactly." Uhura lit the carbide stove Sanner had cobbled together and handed it to Sulu, since he needed its warmth most. He took it awkwardly with his left hand, then brought his right forearm around to steady it with a look of grim determination, as if he'd already come to terms with the need to relearn all the mechanics of motion. "We left survey teams here to explore and catalog this planet—Tlaoli 4—while we went on to Psi 2000. That was the blue planet you remembered self-destructing before you could reach it."

Sulu nodded. "If I recall correctly, we lost the research team that was stationed there."

"So did we." Uhura began looking around the shadowed depths of the cavern for the jumble of equipment they'd left behind when they'd climbed the rubble pile and squirmed out the narrow, winding exit. Had that only been a few hours ago? It seemed like a previous lifetime, now. "In our timeline, we had enough time to send a landing party down to the planet to try and locate them. The landing party caught the virus that had already killed the researchers. It made them—" She broke off, searching for a word that could encompass both the mischievous antics and maniacal acts that the Psi 2000 virus had made various *Enterprise* crew members perform over the past few days.

"Loony," said Dr. McCoy, coming back with the emergency blankets they'd dropped beside the alien healing chamber. "One of 'em locked himself inside the engine room and shut the warp core down for eighteen hours."

"With the planet about to explode at any minute?" Sulu whistled softly as he followed them toward the piles of stacked crates and packs. "What did you do?"

"Captain Kirk and Mr. Spock figured out how to intermix our stocks of matter and antimatter, and cold-start the engines." Uhura bent down to rummage through one of the open crates, looking for rope. She found some and began stringing it from the rough wall of equipment to a nearby travertine pillar. "That worked, but it accidentally threw the *Enterprise* backward in time. We didn't want to confuse the first version of ourselves by reporting to our next assignment early, so we came here instead to repair the ship's engines and help the survey teams we'd left on Tlaoli finish up their work."

"So how did you find this alien transporter that sends people back and forth through time?"

"By accident." Uhura finished knotting the ropes around the column, then propped them up with a surveying rod to support the weight of the emergency blankets. "The surveyors we left behind here found some ancient wrecks of starships. They suspected there might be a natural deposit of transperiodic elements underground creating a space warp in this area, and they came down here to see if they could find it. Instead, they stumbled across an ancient alien installation that drained all the power from their lights and instruments, and stranded them here in the dark. They'd already been trapped for several hours when the *Enterprise* got back into the system."

"So you brought another group down to rescue them." Sulu gave the heater he held an awkward shake and listened to the rattle of carbide rocks inside it, then sniffed at the odor of acetylene gas. "Using primitive chemical combustion lamps?"

"That's right. The alien devices down here drained

all our electromagnetic power sources. We needed something that didn't run on dilithium fuel cells." Uhura draped one of the emergency blankets over the ropes to form a triangular ceiling, then hung the others along the remaining sides. The metallic fabric had an annoying tendency to slither off the ropes until she figured out how to weld it to itself with quick touches from her helmet's hot metal flame reflector. "We found the stranded survey team, but when we tried to beam out, the alien device drained all the power from the *Enterprise*. That seemed to charge up the device enough to actually start moving people around." She held up the last blanket for McCoy and Sulu to step inside the makeshift tent, then picked up some emergency rations she'd found and followed them through. "We thought they were just moving through space."

"But now that you've seen me, you think they were moving through time instead," Sulu said. "Or through alternate dimensions."

"Yes."

Silence followed that exchange, as if its implications were so profound and bewildering that words couldn't immediately grapple with them. In silence, Uhura handed out the ration sticks she'd found while McCoy silently spread the last emergency blanket across the cold travertine cave floor. Sulu settled down cross-legged on it, looking as relaxed as if he were sitting in a padded captain's chair. From the weather-beaten look of his purple and green camouflage jacket, Uhura suspected he'd spent the past few weeks in just this kind of rough accommodation.

"This isn't too bad," McCoy said at last. Uhura knew he must be referring to the quick buildup of warmth inside their silver-walled shelter, since he couldn't possibly mean the desiccated protein stick he held clenched between his teeth like a pipe stem. "Now, exactly what do we need to figure out about our past histories?"

"Point of divergence," Uhura said.

"Overlap," Sulu said.

They glanced at each other for a moment, a distinctly measuring exchange. Back in his own place and time, Uhura recalled, Hikaru Sulu had been the ship's captain and she merely one of his subordinates. But they were in her time here, and until Captain Kirk was reunited with the rest of the landing party, Uhura was officially the officer in charge. Nevertheless, there was no reason to create a command conflict with a man so many years her senior in Starfleet, a man who'd been yanked out of his own time and place through no fault of his own.

"We can keep track of both as we go along," she offered, and saw Sulu smile gently at her, as if she'd been an ensign who'd just answered a tough question correctly. Perhaps after knowing another version of her for twenty years, that was how she seemed to him now. "Um—where should we start?"

"Let's try some major historical milestones," said McCoy around a mouthful of ration stick. "Did you have a Battle of Cheron in your history, Captain Sulu?"

"When Earth defeated the Romulan Empire back in 2160," Sulu said, nodding. "A year later, the United Federation of Planets was established. Was there a Battle at Donatu V in your timeline?"

"Yep. In 2242, about three years before I entered college," McCoy said. "It was our last major run-in with the Klingons."

"That was true in my timeline, until 2273," Sulu said. "The Klingons weren't really friendly with us before that, but we weren't at war with them until after the Gorn invasion."

Uhura was still trying to locate the point at which the older Sulu's history diverged from hers. "In 2266, you were serving aboard the *Enterprise* with me and Dr. McCoy?"

"Yes. You and I were part of her crew when she left spacedock in 2264, under the command of Captain Marshall Hoffman. Dr. McCoy joined us a year or so later, when Dr. Piper left for a research position back on Earth. Does that sound right to you?"

"Everything except for the captain's name." McCoy grimaced and put down his protein stick half-eaten. "If we *are* from alternate dimensions, then they must be pretty damn parallel."

"And if we're from the same dimension, then the only discrepancy so far seems to be the absence of Captain Kirk," Uhura said. "At least, until this Gorn invasion you've been talking about. When did that happen?"

"Stardate 6047.9, Earth year 2269." The older

Sulu's voice deepened a little, as if that date had been etched so deeply into his memory that he couldn't even say it without emotion. "The *Enterprise* was in spacedock for refitting by then...not that it would have mattered. The other starships did what they could, but there wasn't much anyone in space could do." Sulu lifted his right arm as if to rub at his face with fingers he no longer had. He winced and put it back down into his lap, covering the healed end with his left hand. "Sorry," he said again.

"Nothing there you need to be sorry about, son," McCoy said, although Uhura suspected he and Sulu were now almost the same age. "We'll get you fitted with a good mechanical prosthetic just as soon as we get back aboard the *Enterprise*. But who *are* these Gorn you keep talking about?"

Sulu blinked at them across the makeshift tent, as if it was a question he could barely comprehend. Then he shook his head in mild self-disgust. "That's right, you haven't met them yet. And maybe you never will...but we did, back in 2267. It was our first contact, both with the Gorn and a more advanced race called the Metrons. The Gorn were hostile to us from the start—they decoyed *Enterprise* into sending a landing party down to a planet called Cestus III, where they'd already destroyed a Federation outpost. We fought them there and won, but when we pursued them, they fled through Metron space.

"I don't know if the Gorn were trying to throw us off their trail or get us in trouble with the Metrons, but either way it didn't work. The Metrons caught us both and decided to resolve our conflict with a hand-to-hand battle. Just the Gorn captain against our captain." Sulu's lips quirked, as if his memories of that encounter weren't exactly glorious. "We'd lost Captain Hoffman by then, in a nasty run-in we had with the Romulans that nearly got the *Enterprise* destroyed. There wasn't anyone in the quadrant due for a starship promotion, so Commodore Mendez gave Gary Mitchell a brevet-command and we were stuck with him for the next six months." He glanced up at them. "You said he was already dead in your timeline?"

Uhura nodded. "It was early in our five-year mission. We found an ancient recorder buoy and went to investigate what had happened to the ship that left it there, the *S.S. Valiant*. That didn't happen in your timeline?"

The lines on the older pilot's face deepened in frowning concentration, as if it were an effort to reach so far back into his memory. "I think I remember us finding the recorder buoy," he said at last. "But Captain Hoffman decided it wasn't worth investigating because we were too close to the galactic rim."

"And Captain Kirk decided that it *was* worth investigating." Uhura exchanged thoughtful glances with McCoy. Little by little, the alternate history this version of Sulu remembered was starting to make some sense to her. "So, in your timeline Gary Mitchell was in command of the *Enterprise* and had to fight the Gorn. Did he lose?"

"No, he won." Sulu's voice deepened in distaste. "He buried the Gorn captain alive, throwing rocks down on top of him after he was caught and helpless in a pit trap Mitchell had dug. The Metrons showed us the whole thing—and they showed it to the Gorn ship, too."

"So the Gorn wanted vengeance?" guessed McCoy.

"For one dead captain?" Sulu snorted. "No, that probably seemed like perfectly normal warfare to them. What the Gorn wanted vengeance for was what happened to them after the fight was over. The Metrons told us that whichever race lost the fight would be banned from space forever. We didn't find out until later just how they meant to do it. Apparently, after Mitchell killed the Gorn captain, the Metrons destroyed every Gorn spaceship in existence—along with all their crews. Then they locked the Gorn down on their colonies and home planet, and kept them there with force fields too powerful for anyone to break into or out of."

"Then how were the Gorn able to invade the Federation?" the doctor demanded, incredulous.

"We didn't know that for a very long time," Sulu admitted. "All we knew at first was that the Gorn were taking over our outer colonies without traveling through space to do it. They were coming through some kind of energy portals, a new planet-to-planet transporter system they either invented or discovered—"

"A transporter system like this one?" Uhura asked in dismay. "If they found some other part of this alien device, maybe they were able to figure out—"

She stopped because Sulu was already shaking his head at her. *"Not* like this one," he said grimly. "I came out of this one healed. No human being who's ever tried going through a Gorn portal has come out alive." He moved his right arm again, this time cradling it in his left so he could rub awkwardly at the amputated wrist. From the compassionate look on McCoy's face, Uhura suspected the former pilot was feeling phantom pain through severed nerve endings. "Going through their portals was the first thing we tried, when we finally realized how the Gorn were moving their armies from planet to planet. We sent platoons of soldiers through after them, but not a single one survived the trip. Only aliens built like the Gorn and the Klingons can go through and survive, and even 10 percent of them die in the process. The fatality rate is 50 percent for aliens like the Vulcans and Orions, and 100 percent for humans."

"I'm starting to see why you've been at war with the Gorn for twenty years," McCoy said, frowning.

Sulu nodded. "We couldn't even begin to fight them until they finally moved back out into space. Before that, we were always sending ships and troops too late to make a difference. By the time we got the distress call, the Gorn would already have hundreds of thousands of troops occupying a planet. It would take years to dislodge them after that, if we could

manage it at all." His face tightened, as if what he had
to say next was so hard that he couldn't trust himself
to get through it without steeling himself. "We lost
entire branches of the service, and millions of civilian
lives. We lost most of the planets the Gorn attacked.
And if nothing changes about the situation, in the
next year or two I think we're going to lose the war."

An appalled silence followed his words. It was
hard for Uhura, serving at a time when the dangers of
space lay only at the far edges of the Federation, to
get beyond a stunned feeling that the future this Sulu
described was simply impossible. But there was no
disbelieving the grief that deepened the creases on
his timeworn face. She cast around for something,
anything, that might alleviate it.

"Hikaru, if you're not from an alternate dimension,
then maybe your timeline shouldn't have been like
that. If we can figure out how to put Captain Kirk
back where he should have been and fix whatever
went wrong in the past, then maybe none of the future you know will have to happen."

"That would be...nice." Sulu gave her a crooked,
bittersweet smile, so unlike the flashing fearless grin
of his younger self that Uhura almost didn't recognize him. "But after what I've seen for the past
twenty years, you'll have to forgive me if I don't really believe it will come true. And that means you've
got to do more than just figure out how to find this
lost captain of yours. You've *got* to get me back to the
place you took me from."

McCoy squinted at him through the flickering carbide light. "But when you first saw us—didn't you say you thought you had just died there?"

"Yes," Sulu said. "I still have to go back."

"Even if it means going back to certain death?" Uhura asked.

"Yes." Sulu lifted his amputated wrist for them to see, holding it up without self-consciousness for the first time. "If I had succeeded in detonating that pulse bomb where I wanted to, this would have been the best thing that ever happened to me. But I know I didn't. You have to send me back to Basaraba, so I can try again."

"Why?" McCoy demanded.

"Because *my* entire future depends on it," the older man snapped. He paused, eyeing their uncomprehending faces, then took a sharp and rasping breath. "God help me, if I'm in a Gorn torture cell right now and this is all a hallucination, I'm going to wish I really was dead. But if you are from the past, I have to make you understand where I was when this time machine of yours grabbed me. And why you *have* to get me back there again.

"I told you the *Enterprise* was stuck in spacedock when the Gorn invaded. Starfleet Command split up her crew and assigned us to a raft of older battleships and scout ships that they brought back into service, mostly to ferry troops from one invaded planet to the next. You and I and Chekov got a lightweight little frigate called *Hotspur* that was assigned to drop the first advance parties on invaded planets. We were given a crew of academy cadets and brand-new ensigns, and we managed to keep most of them alive, at least until the space battles started up again.

"After the Gorn took over most of our outlying planets, they started trying to close down Federation trade routes, hoping they could starve the better-defended inner planets into submission. We used the *Hotspur* for years to run the blockade, breaking holes in the line for cargo ships to pass through. But after the Klingons attacked us, too, it was all-out war in space from then on. And the whole time, the Gorn were still using their damned portals to grab a planet here, a military station there. Our scientists had been studying them every way they could, trying to find out how they worked and whether we could disrupt them. It was hard even getting close to them, and it took two decades before we finally found out what their Achilles heel was. We did find it, though, at last. *We* found it, Uhura."

The emphasis in Sulu's final statement was unmistakable. Uhura stared at him, feeling her breath catch in her throat even though the Uhura who'd helped achieve that breakthrough was part of a future she hoped she'd never live to see. "What was it?"

"A hub," Sulu said with fierce satisfaction. "A single central hub portal that every Gorn soldier had to go through, every time the portals were used. And all we needed to do, to cripple the entire Gorn invasion, was to destroy it."

* * *

For a long time after the shuttle crashed, Sulu just sat in the pilot's seat and listened to the soft pelting of rain against the hull. He told himself he was lying low in case any of this alien planet's guardians had been left behind to watch for survivors. But with a rainy gray-violet dusk settling over the rain forest and hundreds of meters of treetop canopy shielding him overhead, the probability of being seen was quickly approaching zero. Deep inside, Sulu knew he just didn't trust himself to make sensible decisions right now. The months he'd spent on the *Enterprise* had taught him to recognize the little tremors in his hands and the swift frantic way his thoughts were spinning as a result of too much adrenaline in a body already reeling from too much fatigue.

He might not have been so wary of making decisions in this state if he didn't have such vivid memories of the bitterly cold vigil he'd stood on Alfa 117 a month ago while the *Enterprise* repaired her malfunctioning transporters. Sulu distinctly remembered thinking at one point toward the end of the ordeal that it would be a good idea to start walking down to the planet's equator. If his feet hadn't been so numb with cold and frostbite that his very first step landed him flat on his back and knocked some sense into him, he might have actually started the 23,000-kilometer trek and missed getting beamed out with the rest of the landing party.

So right now, Sulu was forcing himself just to sit and watch the darkness settle and rain sluice down the *Drake*'s impact-starred cockpit windows. Pelting hard against the shuttle's duranium-clad nose when the wind drove it and splashing soft as poured milk when it didn't, the sound reminded him so much of wet San Francisco nights spent on his great-great-grandfather's sailboat that he kept expecting to smell salt air and the delicate tang of the old man's jasmine tea. What he got instead was the pungent odor of an alien rain forest, seeping in through the rents where the nacelles had been torn away from the shuttle's hull.

It was a thick and complicated smell, compounded of wet moss, crushed and stripped tree bark, and some kind of night-blooming flowers whose scent was magnolia-sweet and citrus-sharp at the same time. It was an odor the botany enthusiast in Sulu might have enjoyed under other circumstances, but right now all it did was remind him that he was stranded on a completely unknown planet in a completely unknown part of the galaxy. He had never felt farther away from San Francisco, or, for that matter, from the entire rest of his life.

The smell of the rain forest wasn't the only thing coming into the shuttle. A glittering film of small flying insects gathered over Sulu's control panel, apparently attracted to the feverish blinking of the mechanical failure lights. They didn't seem inclined to bite him, but they did keep getting in his eyes and nose and ears. Sulu put up with them as long as he could, then cursed and fled back into the passenger hold. Its steady emergency lighting didn't seem to attract as many of the gnatlike creatures, and the spill of emergency supplies from the shattered shell of one bulkhead reminded him that there was work he could do here before he had to make any irrevocable decisions about his future.

The *Drake* had been stripped of nonessential equipment before its final trip down to Tlaoli, in preparation for evacuating a landing party that nearly exceeded its cargo weight limit. But Starfleet safety regulations decreed that all shuttles carried in their bulkhead storage an emergency medical kit and enough water and supplies to survive being stranded in space for three days. Since the *Drake* normally carried a crew of four, that meant there were plenty of supplies for Sulu to sort through.

The crash had burst two of the four water containers and drenched one of the food packs, which meant Sulu had to spread the individually wrapped rations out to dry on the shuttle's bare floor. At first, he set aside all the ones that had been crushed or whose plastifoil wrappers had been torn open. After seeing how much of his potential food supply he was losing, however, Sulu forced himself to eat whatever he could extricate from the broken containers. His initial intention was just to make some use of food that would be spoiled by tomorrow, but after a few minutes he realized that the salty cold mush of unheated stew and paper-flavored sticks of dehydrated protein felt remarkably good to his grinding stomach. Several crushed remnants of energy bars later, Sulu's tremors had subsided and he found himself thinking clearly again.

Wherever he had been flung by Tlaoli's strange alien force field, his first duty was to get back to the Federation and to Starfleet. Since the *Drake* was no longer spaceworthy, there was no way Sulu could make the trip back on his own, even if he could somehow figure out where in space he was. But the crashed cargo shuttle still had two useful things left in it: an intact warp core and a subspace communicator. The latter had been so completely useless back on Tlaoli that Sulu had turned it off to free himself of the distracting squawk of subspace interference. In the shock of his arrival and subsequent crash, it hadn't occurred to him to turn it back on again.

Scooping up a last mangled pack of carbohydrate wafers and a cannister of sterile water to wash them down with, Sulu headed back into the swarming fog of insects that filled the cockpit. The shuttle's designers hadn't thought to include an insect-repellent field generator in the emergency cache, probably because when they'd thought of emergencies they'd envisioned the shuttle drifting helplessly in deep space rather than wrecked in a primeval rain forest. But Sulu had armed himself from the first-aid kit with a can of disinfectant spray that had a sharp, unpleasant smell. He used it to blow the film of gnats off the communicator controls, then doused himself thoroughly before he sat back in his seat. The insects crowded back against the windows of the cockpit, a

spangled and gauzy veil that almost obscured the outside dark and splattering rain.

Sulu brushed a few drowned gnats off the communicator's display panel, then switched the unit on and
watched it power itself up. The frequency monitor ran
through a spectrum of subspace channels, spiking several times to indicate it had detected communicator sig-
nals at that wavelength. Sulu wondered whether he
should be reassured or worried that this planet's inhabitants had subspace technology equivalent to the Federation's. He knew he wasn't in the territory of Starfleet's
known enemies—the attack ships that had chased him
hadn't looked anything like the Klingons' claw-shaped
fighters, or the ramshackle pirate fleets of Orion. But
Sulu had no idea what Romulan ships might look like,
after the centuries of mutual avoidance that had passed
since Earth's last hostile encounter with those mysterious aliens. For all he knew, he could be sitting on one of
the Romulans' legendary twin homeworlds right now.

It was that unpleasant thought which inspired
Sulu, when the communicator had finished its scan
and sat waiting for further instructions, to punch in
his security clearance code before he did anything
else. Then he painstakingly programmed the communicator to broadcast a coded and anonymous Starfleet
distress call at the maximum level of security. It took
him several minutes to do what Uhura could probably
have done in seconds, but at last he sat back and
watched his signal go out on a restricted channel hidden in the shoulder of ionized helium's discharge

band. To anyone scanning randomly across the frequency spectrum, that short "officer-in-distress" code would look like nothing more than natural subspace noise. Only a Starfleet base that monitored those restricted frequencies and knew how to decode the seemingly meaningless static on them would understand Sulu's cry for help.

He sighed and immediately wished he hadn't. His eau de disinfectant had faded away, and the air around him once again glittered with tiny translucent bodies. Sulu was reaching for the spray cannister when a loud voice from the communicator jerked him upright in surprise. It wasn't preceded by an official Starfleet hailing tone and its owner didn't even bother to identify himself. All he did was say one incredulous and utterly unexpected word.

"Sulu?"

Chapter Three

"LET ME GUESS," said Dr. McCoy, in the hissing silence of the carbide-lit tent. "You were trying to destroy this central hub and stop the Gorn from invading the Federation when we hauled you out of your timeline and into ours."

"Yes." The glint of triumph faded from Sulu's lined face, and left him looking older and more tired than before. He glanced down at what was left of his right arm. "Trying, but not succeeding. The Gorn hub is probably still there and still working."

"What happened?" Uhura asked.

"We were ferrying troops to a newly invaded Vulcan colony when we ran across a Romulan battleship and attacked it." The former helmsman said those words so offhandedly that Uhura felt almost jolted.

She had to keep telling herself that for this Sulu, all-out war had become a way of life. "It ran for refuge to a minor planet near the galactic fringe. When we chased after it, we got attacked by so many Gorn fighters that we knew the planet wasn't one of their normal colony worlds. We pretended to veer off, then circled back and saw the installation they were guarding. It looked like it could be the portal hub, so we hit it with all the anti-invasion troops we were ferrying to Xlamat, in a surprise attack." Sulu's lips tightened to a slash of remembered pain. "They were slaughtered down to a man."

Uhura let a moment of merciful silence pass before she spoke again. "What did you do after that?"

Sulu sighed. "We tried taking the *Hotspur* low into the atmosphere and firing every weapon we had—and by that point in the war, as you can imagine, we had an awful lot of firepower. It never even shook the towers above the fortress, much less the main underground portal. After that, there was only one thing left to do. We sacrificed the *Hotspur* to catch a Gorn shuttle and crash-landed them both, to make them think we all were dead." Sulu glanced up at her with another of those strange, bittersweet smiles, as if the years of war had taught him to find a dark thread of humor even in disaster. "Actually, most of us *were* dead by then. There was only a skeleton bridge crew left—you, me, Chekov. While we repaired the Gorn shuttle, we took turns watching Tesseract Fortress and listening to its communicator chatter. We noticed after a while that there weren't just Gorns showing up around that place—all the races they'd allied with or enslaved were there, too, massing and organizing for some major deployment. Maybe an invasion of Vulcan, we thought, or even of Earth. We waited as long as we could, but we didn't want to let them start sending that army through the portals if we could help it.

"So we salvaged our last pulse bomb from the wreck of the *Hotspur* and infiltrated Tesseract Fortress. We suspected the reason our previous attacks had failed was because the portal was generating a subspace force field so powerful that it actually protected itself from attack. Once we got inside the fortress walls, we were going to take our pulse bomb into the portal and detonate it from inside while Chekov—made a distraction."

Sulu's steady voice didn't falter as he recounted his own suicidal part in that final plan, Uhura noticed, but it did when he tried to gloss over the grim reality of what his subordinate had done. She reminded herself again about all the hellish years of war this man had endured, and said nothing. Dr. McCoy wasn't quite so tactful.

"You let that boy deliberately sacrifice himself?"

"Not such a boy in my time as in yours, Doctor. And by 2296, every officer in Starfleet would have sacrificed themselves if it could save another million civilian lives. I just wish it could have been that simple."

"You never made it into the portal with the pulse bomb?"

"No," Sulu said regretfully. "God knows the Gorn transfer enough weapons through that hub during their invasions, but they must have detectors to pick up activated ones. They slammed their security fields down on us before we even got close to the gate, then raked us with explosive projectile weapons. I saw Uhura get hit—felt the bomb get shot out of my hand and saw it start to ignite—and then I was here."

Sulu stopped speaking, and this time both McCoy and Uhura let the silence stretch out undisturbed until the older pilot himself broke it.

"Now do you understand why I have to go back?" he asked, pinning Uhura with a sharp, direct look that reminded her of Captain Kirk. "If my future really is your future, then the fate of my Federation and yours depends on you getting me back through this damned time transporter of yours."

Sulu reached through a glistening film of insects to activate the *Drake*'s communicator, then paused with his finger just a centimeter away. Was this a trap? Could the aliens who chased him away from the military fortress have somehow learned his name, telepathically or through some exotic technology that he couldn't even begin to comprehend?

"Sulu," the communicator said again, impatiently. "I know you're the only one who could have flown that shuttle, much less sent out that old Starfleet emergency signal. If you're alive out there, say something!"

Sulu eyed the communicator in surprise. The threadlike flash of its frequency monitor told him this signal was coming in on the same restricted and high-security Starfleet channel he'd used to broadcast his coded distress call, but that wasn't what made him take a deep breath and complete his motion toward the activation switch. Maybe he was wrong, but he couldn't imagine any aliens, telepathic or otherwise, who would bother to speak English with a Russian accent.

"Sulu here," he said into the communicator. "Who is this?"

"Bok spasibo!" said the thankful voice on the other end of the channel. It didn't sound much like a name, but since Sulu didn't know what else it could be, he decided not to make an issue of it for now. "Where are you now, Captain?"

Captain?

"I'm still in the shuttle," Sulu said, cautiously. For all that the man he was talking to seemed to know him, there was still something very odd about this conversation. "I—uh—landed it in the rain forest. Where are you?"

"Flying low over the Serippat Hills, with the cloaking device engaged and no Gorn in sight," the other voice said. "Keep talking and I'll triangulate on your signal. Is…is Uhura still with you?"

Sulu paused once again with his finger centimeters from the communicator controls, this time ready to break contact. What stopped him wasn't the familiar name of his *Enterprise* crewmate, but the unmistakable tension in the other man's voice when he asked about her. That couldn't be part of some alien plot to lure him out of hiding...even if the aliens could read his mind and know that Uhura had been down on Tlaoli with him just before he disappeared, there was no particular reason for them to pretend to be fearful about her. To the best of Sulu's knowledge, she was still safe and sound.

"No, she's not here," he said. "She's back at the base camp on Tlaoli."

There was a long moment of silence. "What?"

The mixture of bewilderment and suspicion in that reply sounded so exactly like what Sulu was feeling himself that he was almost tempted to laugh. Clearly, whoever he was talking to found this conversation about as confusing as he did... and suddenly, Sulu's overtired mind made a connection between this gruff, Russian-accented voice and the self-conscious young ensign he'd met just before he'd taken off to look for Captain Kirk on Tlaoli.

"Is this Chekov?" he demanded.

"Of course it's Chekov," was the sharp and far from self-conscious reply. "What kind of a stupid question is that? Sulu, are you wounded? Did they spray you with any of their drugs?"

"No," said Sulu. "But something's not right here."

The communicator crackled, but it took Sulu a moment to recognize it as the sound of mirthless laughter. "Nothing's been right for a long time now. Stay where you are. I have your location fixed now, and there's still no sign of Gorn. I'll set down in the nearest clearing and come get you."

Sulu opened his mouth to ask Chekov who the Gorn were, how the young ensign had come to this alien planet, and where he had obtained the craft he was flying. But the thread of light marking the open high-security channel between them died abruptly back to its baseline and left him sitting in the rain and darkness, wondering what to do next.

The most prudent reaction would probably be to evacuate the shuttle, but that would put Sulu out in the darkness of an alien forest with very little equipment and even less idea of what he was supposed to do next. He reminded himself that his goal right now was simply to get back to the Federation, which made the presence of a fellow Starfleet officer on this planet a godsend. While there was something odd and almost anomalous about the way Chekov had talked to him, at the moment that familiar Russian-accented voice was his only tie back to Tlaoli and the *Enterprise*.

But the more he thought about it, the more troubled Sulu found himself by Chekov's presence here. He'd last seen the young ensign heading off into the Tlaoli karstlands in dogged pursuit of their lost captain, just minutes before Sulu had encountered the windstorm that transported him here. Even if Chekov had somehow gotten caught up in that same alien force, how could he have arrived on this planet so far in advance of Sulu that he not only had found a shuttle to fly, but also had learned the names of the aliens and the landforms and acquainted himself with strange technologies Sulu had never heard of? It didn't make any sense....

Until Sulu remembered that Chekov was the one other person, besides Captain Kirk, who had previously been abducted by the strange alien force fields of Tlaoli.

Uhura had said the young Russian had been transported a short distance through the caves, and that nothing more had happened to him. But maybe that wasn't true. Maybe the alien transportation device on Tlaoli sent everyone it caught to this distant alien planet. Or maybe—Sulu had an even worse but chillingly logical thought—maybe the alien transporter just sent *copies* of the people it caught. Sulu had met Chekov after he'd been transported through the caves, after all, and the Russian couldn't have been both here and on Tlaoli at the same time. It was far more likely that he and Sulu had both been scanned and duplicated here, the same way Captain Kirk had been duplicated aboard the *Enterprise* a few months ago when the ship's transporter malfunctioned and split him into two complimentary selves.

If his theory was right, Sulu thought, there should be a duplicate copy of Captain Kirk here as well. He repressed an urge to issue a wide-band call for the captain on his communicator, knowing it would be more likely to attract the attention of hostile aliens—these Gorn Chekov had mentioned—than to make contact with a man who might or might not even be present on the planet. He would mention his duplication theory to Chekov when the young man came to meet him, Sulu thought as he waved a veil of gnats away from his face. Then, if they really did seem to be just copies of their original selves, they could worry together about what to do next.

Sulu should have realized how much the soft pelting of the rain against the shuttle's hull muffled any other sounds from reaching it, but he was so busy thinking about the unpleasant aspects of his duplication theory that the footfall he heard inside the cargo's hold took him completely by surprise. He spun around in his pilot's seat and started to get up, but the unmistakable snout of a metal weapon poked him in the chest before he could take a step. Sulu sank back into his seat, blood running cold as a scarred stranger's face followed the weapon into the cockpit.

"You," said the older man in a murderous-sounding but eerily familiar Russian voice, "are not Captain Sulu."

"No," Sulu said, when he could finally manage to speak. "I'm Lieutenant Hikaru Sulu, helmsman of the *U.S.S. Enterprise.*"

That answer, which he expected to be greeted by either a growl of rage or a snort of disdain, instead got him an impassive and intent stare. "Helmsman of the *Enterprise?*" the other man asked slowly. "Right now?"

Sulu glanced around the insect-filled shuttle and couldn't restrain a small, wry smile. "Well, not right now. But usually, yes." He glanced back up, trying to see past the gleam of the weapon to its owner's shadowed eyes. "And you?"

"You don't know me?"

There was no discernable emotion in that blunt question, but Sulu still felt a little guilty when he shook his head.

"I'm Commander Pavel Chekov, first officer of the *Hotspur.*" The older man lowered the weapon and took another step into the blinking glow of the cockpit's instrument lights. Sulu tried hard to match his face to that of the young ensign he'd just met on Tlaoli, but between the ugly scarring and the gauntness, even the dark eyes barely looked familiar. "You're younger than I remember ever seeing you," Chekov said somberly. "So you probably don't even know me yet. But twenty years ago, I was—or I will be—your navigator on board the *Enterprise.*"

"Lieutenant, hey, Lieutenant Uhura!" The distant shout from outside the walls of their shelter broke the strained silence that had fallen after Sulu's final grim words. "Lieutenant, you'll never guess what's going on down in that ice cave!"

Uhura lifted a corner of an emergency blanket and felt a rush of cold cavern air displace the warmth that had built up inside the insulated space. The nanofibers of her caving suit promptly expanded to compensate for the change in temperature, but she could see Sulu wince and hug his blood-stained camouflage jacket tighter around him with his left hand. Uhura motioned for him and Dr. McCoy to stay inside, then let the blanket fall behind her as she ducked out into the larger, column-filled cavern. It took her a moment to locate the glow of Sanner's carbide lamp. It was dim as a firefly and far across the cavernous darkness, but it skipped and leaped toward her with the cave geologist's typical energy.

"There you are! With all those reflective blankets you hung up, I couldn't see anybody's light....I thought maybe you guys had left without me." Sanner condensed from a vague shadow beneath his helmet light into something so formless and white that he looked like a ghostly apparition floating toward her. Uhura peered at him as he got closer and saw that his cave jumper was thickly furred with extruded hoarfrost, as if it had gotten completely drenched and then frozen. His helmet was covered with a glittering rime of ice.

"What happened to you?" she exclaimed.

Sanner's grin flashed in the darkness. "Just what would happen to anyone stupid enough to walk under a waterfall in the dark. I was keeping my light turned off as much as I could—"

"Get inside," Uhura ordered, pulling the emergency blanket up and waving the geologist beneath it. He shed his ice-crusted pack as he went, then hunkered down near the little carbide heater and began stripping off his frozen gloves, talking the entire time.

"—since I figured I'd rather hit a rock, or even a

waterfall than run into that alien force field without seeing it. Lieutenant Uhura, did you know there were blue emergency lights in all those alien conduits down there?"

Uhura finished resealing the tent walls behind her and came to join the others, settling down at a safe distance from Sanner and the pool of melt water already forming around him. "I noticed there were lights in the walls," she said, remembering the eerie glow she'd seen during their tense retreat from the ice cave. She'd assumed it was part and parcel of the same mysterious force field that had swept away Captain Kirk and Ensign Chekov. Sanner's more prosaic explanation, that the aliens who built and used this place would have needed to illuminate the dark corridors they made, had never even occurred to her. "Were they bright enough for you to keep your carbide turned off all the time?"

"Not really." Sanner shed his helmet and shook shards of ice off the collar of his uniform. "Obviously. But I left the carbide turned off anyway, so I could spot that force field from as far away as possible."

"Where was it this time?"

"I don't know! I never saw it, because there was too much water running in the corridor to get down that far." Sanner gazed expectantly across the tent toward Uhura, as if what he had just said should have meant something to her. Her face must have shown her blank incomprehension, because the geologist smacked his empty gloves across his knee as if that could pound the significance of his words home to her. What it actually did was splatter him with droplets of melting ice. *"Water,* Lieutenant! Running down the corridors, making a waterfall through the hole in the roof where that kid Chekov and Captain Kirk fell through...."

"Oh!" Uhura's eyes widened as she finally realized what he meant. "The ice is melting! The caves must be getting warmer again."

"Precisely, as Mr. Spock would say." With a grimace, Sanner blew on his fingers. His bare hands were now wetter and probably colder than they had been before he'd stripped off his waterproof gloves. "This upper cave is the coldest part of the whole system now, trust me. I was soaking wet for fifteen minutes on the way back, but I didn't start freezing until I was halfway up the spiral that leads here."

"Stick your hands up your sleeves," McCoy suggested. "That'll get 'em dry again."

"Thanks." Sanner wriggled his fingers under the edges of his jumper sleeves, and a sheen of extruded water promptly appeared on the outside of the cloth as it wicked the cold water away from his skin. "The farther down you go toward the ice cave, the warmer it gets," he told Uhura enthusiastically. "You can see by the way the fog's building up down there that it's the walls of the conduits that are getting warmer, not just the air flowing through them."

"So what does that mean?" McCoy asked. "If

you're trying to convince us to stay down here and do some more caving, Zap—"

"No, no! This tells us something important about energy consumption." Sanner waved his gloves for emphasis, scattering them all with ice-cold drops of water. "When I first heard how the *Enterprise* lost so much power trying to beam us out of here, I started to wonder what was going on down here, energy-wise. I mean, if this place really did have its own transperiodic energy source, it wouldn't need to drain power from us, would it? It would create *heat* as a by-product, not cold, the same way dilithium crystals do when they generate a warp field. But instead, the temperature dropped every time we lost power down here. And I think that means Tlaoli is exactly as energy depleted as we first thought when we surveyed it. The only way the alien transporter can be activated is by stealing energy from any outside sources it comes into contact with."

"Like the power cells in our tricorders and phasers," Uhura said when Sanner finally had to pause to take a breath.

McCoy grunted. "Or the power storage banks of *Enterprise,* after it made contact with that transporter beam."

"Anything with electrical currents flowing through it," Sanner agreed. "I have no idea how the energy gets taken…maybe through some sophisticated subspace magnetic fields, maybe some other kind of alien physics we don't understand yet. But I'm betting that it takes that machine a long time to build up the energy it needs to activate a transfer. And in the meantime, it has to store its power somewhere."

"That would make sense," Uhura said. "But what does the cold have to do with it?"

"Isn't it obvious?" Sanner said. "The energy storage reaction has to be *endothermic*, Lieutenant. The more energy that gets put into the system, the more heat the system absorbs from the ambient environment." The cave geologist waved his gloves again, this time up at the shadowy rock ceiling that loomed above their sheltering emergency blankets. "That might have been okay a million years ago when this place was basking in sunshine, but now that it's buried underground, it's not so good. Rock is an *awful* conductor of heat, so nothing flows in to replace what the energy storage reaction takes out. The result is an instant deep freeze whenever the machine starts charging itself up."

Uhura took a deep breath of comprehension. "Then when it starts warming up again...does that mean the device has taken its energy out of storage and used it?"

"Bingo!" Sanner rocked back on his heels, looking enormously pleased with himself. "Energy consumption has to be the machine's limiting factor, Lieutenant! And the fact that it's still getting warmer in the caves right now means—"

"—that the alien transporter used up all of its energy supply transporting me here," Sulu said. The older man's deep voice sounded composed and thoughtful, as if this scientific puzzle was the only thing he had to worry about right now. Uhura's respect for this future version of Sulu was increasing the longer she knew him, as was her conviction that there must be more to the young helmsman she already knew than an easy smile and an enthusiasm for unusual hobbies. "It *would* need a tremendous amount of power to move someone halfway across the galaxy and backward twenty years in time—"

"—especially since it sent our version of Sulu back the other way!" Sanner finished triumphantly.

Uhura felt her stomach knot up. "We don't know for sure that it did that, Zap. He may have just been transferred to some other part of Tlaoli—"

The scientist started shaking his head before she even finished her sentence. "Not according to my calculations, Lieutenant. I estimated how much power the transporter here could have absorbed from all our dilithium cells and from the *Enterprise.* God only knows how much power it takes to travel through time, but if you assume it's an order of magnitude more than what it would take to go that same distance through space...well, the equation only balanced out if I assumed it was a two-way transfer and the shuttle got sent, too."

"You're forgetting that the alien transporter already used some of its power transporting Captain Kirk and Ensign Chekov," McCoy pointed out.

"No, I'm not," Sanner said indignantly. "It barely needed any power at all to move that kid Chekov around down here. Especially since if he skipped through time at all, it couldn't have been by much.

We've still got pretty much the same Chekov we started out with."

"But probably not the same Kirk," McCoy said. "And we won't know where and when the alien transporter sent him until we find the version that got out of this cave and is wandering around up on the surface somewhere."

"But the important thing," said the older Sulu, "is that the warming of the caves suggests the alien device is no longer charged up or capable of transporting anyone, either to the future or the past. Is that correct?"

"I think so," said Sanner. "I just wish I could have gotten down to the ice cave to make absolutely sure the force field was gone...."

"There's another way we can check on that." Uhura swung around to eye the pile of stacked crates and backpacks she had used as the tent's third wall. One crate in the corner was marked with the Starfleet division symbol she knew better than any other in the service. She wrestled it out from the stack, making the tent sag a little in that corner, then threw open the lid to expose the small, portable communicator inside.

"That won't work," McCoy objected. "If the survey team brought it down with them, its power supply should be drained and dead now."

"It is," Uhura said, seeing the telltale darkness where a status readout should have blinked. She lifted the communicator out from the box anyway. "But we brought the last of Martine's chemical battery packs down here with us. You didn't use them for anything, did you, Zap?"

"Nope." The geologist was already rummaging through his overloaded backpack. "They're in here somewhere, probably all the way at the bottom. There we go."

He handed the old-fashioned chemical battery to Uhura, who had already opened the communicator's cover and pulled out the wires connected to its drained power supply. She twisted them around the terminals of the chemical battery instead, then took a deep breath and slid open the partition that let the old-fashioned chemical reservoirs come into contact and start the flow of electricity. She had no doubt that the alien transporter would soon begin to drain this power supply, just as it had drained all the others they had brought down into these caves. But, in the meantime, they just might have a chance—

"Uhura to *Enterprise*," she said into the communicator, spacing her words for maximum clarity. "Come in, *Enterprise*."

There was a pause whose pure silence seemed almost too good to be true, then Uhura heard the tiny click she was waiting for and began to breathe again.

"*Enterprise* here," said Spock's clear and familiar voice on the other end of the open channel. "A status report would be most welcome, Lieutenant."

Uhura repressed an undignified urge to giggle at the austere hint of reproach coloring the Vulcan's response. "Aye, sir." She gave him a succinct explanation of everything that had happened since her last contact with the ship. "We're still not sure what happened to Captain Kirk," she said at the end. "All we know is that the Sulu we have now never served under him or knew him."

Fear of losing her connection to the ship had made Uhura's explanation so condensed that she wondered if even Spock's superhuman intelligence could grasp all the nuances of it. She waited worriedly, watching the power supply indicator slowly decay on the communicator's status panel, and finally heard McCoy grumble, "Come on, Spock, say something," beneath his breath.

"Report acknowledged, Lieutenant." The Vulcan sounded no different than he had a moment before. "Under the circumstances, it would clearly be too dangerous to beam anyone down to assist you, but we will send another shuttle as soon as possible. What do you estimate the current power supply of the alien transportation device to be?"

"Low, we think, but we haven't been able to make a direct observation." Uhura saw Sanner frantically flapping a piece of paper at her from across the tent and realized it was his topographic map of the overlying karst plateau. "Geologic Specialist Sanner has some information about where the danger levels might be highest."

Sanner scuttled across the tent on his knees and bent over the communicator. "Bearing due south from the highest peak in the southern karst plain—" He rattled off a series of numbers and vectors that made no sense to Uhura. "—keep entirely clear of that area," he concluded. "Have the shuttle approach base camp from the opposite side of the karst plain."

"I believe I can pilot in accordance with those restrictions," Spock said calmly. Uhura opened her mouth, but McCoy was already asking the question she intended to ask, a lot more incredulously than she would have dared.

"Spock, you're not coming down here yourself, are you?"

"Certainly I am, Doctor." That urbane Vulcan voice never expressed any emotion as palpably human as worry, but there was an undertone to it now that was at least reminiscent of that emotion. "There will be an unavoidable delay of approximately thirty minutes while Commander Scott installs magnetic shielding around the warp core and engines of a second cargo shuttle. During that time, you will gather all personnel at the survey team's base camp so that we may begin to analyze and deal with the situation as soon as I arrive. That," he added unnecessarily, "is an order."

"Aye-aye, sir," Uhura said, but McCoy wasn't quite as easily intimidated.

"What's the hurry, Spock?" he demanded. "Is there somewhere else we're supposed to be right now?"

"No, but there is somewhere else that we currently *are*," the science officer replied sharply. "And that *Enterprise*—the one that is supposed to exist at this time and place—has probably already been affected

by the disruptions we have created in the timeline."
Spock's voice became muffled as the chemical battery began to lose its electrical charge, but Uhura still
had no trouble hearing the starkness in his words. "If
something we have done has erased Captain Kirk
from our own past, then the only reason we can remember him now is because we are floating in a bubble of disconnected time caused by our inadvertent
slingshot at Psi 2000. And that bubble is due to rejoin
the main timeline approximately fifty-six hours from
now."

Chapter Four

TLAOLI'S LITTLE LEMON SUN cast a clean, surprisingly hard light over the scrubby plains beyond the karst plateau. It reminded Chekov of summers in Siberia, where the sun could blind you even though the air was cool, and every midge and shrew and snow tern took advantage of the brief season. Only here on Tlaoli, the ground under their feet was hard and dry, not half-frozen beneath a blanket of mud, and there were no clouds to feather the edges of shadows and grant some rest to the eye. By the time the base camp lifted into view on the edge of a pale horizon, Chekov's head hurt and the back of his uniform tunic was scratchy and damp with sweat. He envied Kirk his youth and civilian status—the boy had shouldered out of his shirt half an hour ago, walking bare-chested in the springlike morning with no hint of self-consciousness or impropriety.

"So that's where the rest of them are waiting?"

Kirk had slowed his pace a little, squinting under his shading hand even though the sun was still more behind them than overhead. It was pretense, Chekov knew. An excuse to postpone walking into the camp, where he would only find himself off-balance and outnumbered by adults who knew more about him than he did himself. After three months as the newest kid on an established starship, Chekov understood how he felt. So he let Kirk have the delay. Drawing up alongside, he pretended not to notice Tomlinson's irritation as the rest of the party caught up to them and slowed to a halt.

"They should all be there by now." Although he was really only guessing—he didn't know how long Lieutenant Uhura and Mr. Sanner would be underground. "They'll be relieved that we found you."

The boy nodded, a calm, noncommittal gesture. "Do they know?" he asked. "I mean, do they know about me—that I'm *not*…me?" It was hard enough to think about, let alone try to discuss.

"They know we went out looking for Captain Kirk." Chekov had decided that the easiest way to keep things straight in his own head was to think of them as two distinctly separate people with coincidentally similar names. Remembering his own teen years, he suspected it wasn't that far from the truth. "They don't know yet that we found you instead, but they'll still be glad to see you."

"Why?" The bitterness in young Kirk's tone caught Chekov by surprise. "It's not like I'll be any use on board a starship."

"Don't worry, son." Plastering on one of those stiff, insincere smiles that adults would never tolerate having directed at themselves, Tomlinson reached out to tousle Kirk's hair as he stepped between the boy and Chekov on his way to the front of the group. "We'll make sure you're well taken care of." He cast a disapproving glare at Chekov, just missing Kirk's angry duck out from under his hand as he turned back to his own, more important adult affairs. "Meanwhile, Ensign, we've got a report to make to our commander, so let's get moving, shall we?"

Chekov nodded, but he doubted Tomlinson saw that, either. The lieutenant was already striding toward the base camp, apparently intent on proving that he had a job to do and he knew what it was. The only hint of apology came from Martine as she hurried to follow behind—a quick backward glance and the flash of an embarrassed smile. But she didn't hold up to wait for the others, or say anything to the boy who would one day be her commanding officer.

If he remembers this twenty years from now, you'll never set foot outside the Weapons Room again, Chekov thought. He was surprised Tomlinson couldn't feel the laser burn of the boy's glare between his shoulders. Or maybe he did, and he just didn't think a fourteen-year-old's indignation mattered.

Tomlinson had been irritable ever since Chekov and Kirk rejoined him on the floor of the karst maze. Smith must have explained the circumstances surrounding her separation from Chekov, because the lieutenant only asked them awkwardly, "Everything okay?" without bothering to introduce himself to the boy in Chekov's company or ask for the newcomer's name. Upon being assured that everyone was in one piece and mobile, Tomlinson had stated simply, "We've got a long walk back to the base camp," and started them on their way.

At first, Chekov had assumed his senior officer was angry at him for splitting up with Smith, or for usurping (however unintentionally) Tomlinson's leadership role by being the one to first make contact with Kirk. But as the morning wore on, and Tomlinson's behavior morphed inexpertly from gruff commander to patronizing buddy and back again, Chekov realized that the angry glances and sharp comments flung his way were only fallout from a more generalized unhappiness. It wasn't Chekov who had Tomlinson flustered and unhappy—it was Kirk.

As soon as the thought occurred to him, the evidence was everywhere. The lieutenant almost never made eye contact with Kirk, but when he did, a peculiar expression that was half resentment, half condescension made his eyes and smile seem like parts of two unrelated faces. He hadn't called Kirk by name even once, resorting instead to ridiculous diminutives like "son" and "young man." Chekov wondered if it was just the shock of finding a much-too-young James Kirk at the end of their hunt that had Tomlinson so agitated, or if any teenager would have done the trick.

"Look!" Smith's exclamation caught his attention sufficiently to break his reverie, but she felt the need to swat him repeatedly on the shoulder anyway. Chekov felt a little bit like Kirk as he ducked out from under her blows. "Isn't that the shuttle?" She acknowledged his movement by changing her swat to what was probably supposed to be an apologetic pat, but was obviously too excited to take offense or feel embarrassed. "Doesn't that mean Mr. Sulu's okay after all? Maybe they figured out how the alien transporter works, and now they can use it to put everybody back to where they were!"

Kirk didn't look as pleased by the prospect as Chekov might have expected. He pretended not to notice the question Chekov glanced in his direction, and instead made himself very busy with shaking out his shirt and jamming his arms down the sleeves.

"At ease, Crewman." Tomlinson's attempt to sound mature and unruffled instead came out as weary disappointment. "Lieutenant Sulu was flying the *Drake*. The nose cone says that's the *Herschel*. They must have sent another team down."

Which begged the question: Why? All they'd managed to do so far was lose or strand everyone who'd set foot on this planet. Adding a few more to the tally hardly seemed productive.

A flurry of activity at the edges of the camp made it clear that someone had been watching for their return. Chekov found himself moving a few steps closer to Kirk, feeling Smith pull in just behind his right shoulder, and hoped the boy didn't notice their sudden protectiveness. Chekov wasn't sure what to expect from the landing party—he hadn't expected Tomlinson's strangely hostile reaction to finding the young man—but he knew Kirk didn't need a flood of pity and disappointment the moment he set foot inside their camp. He suddenly wished they'd been able to whisk him in under cover of darkness. Then they could have told everyone what to expect while the boy was still asleep, and given the shock a chance to run its course before parading him around in public.

But even in the most bizarre circumstances, the *Enterprise*'s crew maintained its professionalism and calm. They gathered quietly, clearly studying the boy but not pointing or gasping or uttering cries of alarm. Kirk returned their frankly curious stares stoically. He reminded Chekov of a young prince, facing his subjects for the very first time.

Oddly, it was Tomlinson who saved them from any further awkwardness. "Is Lieutenant Uhura back yet?" He aimed the question at no one in particular, but the older geologist near the front of the group answered pleasantly enough.

"Carolyn has gone to get her." Jaeger smiled at Kirk with the sort of paternal kindness that somehow ceased to be insulting once you were in your sixth decade. "Ah, but this young man will complicate things, I think."

A cool, deep voice beyond Jaeger caught everyone's attention; the small crowd swung about and parted, almost unconsciously clearing a lane for the tall, black-haired officer. "James Kirk, I presume."

For some reason, when Chekov had imagined a new shuttle crew bringing the *Herschel* down to join them, he hadn't expected Commander Spock to be among those on board.

Kirk looked the Vulcan over with only the slightest hint of surprise. "You can call me Jim." It occurred to Chekov that this young Kirk might very well have never met a Vulcan before.

Spock dipped his head minutely. "Very well. I am Commander Spock, first officer of the starship *Enterprise*."

Kirk nodded in return, then, seeming to have come to a sudden decision, he stepped forward and boldly thrust out his hand. "I'm pleased to meet you, sir."

Spock arched one eyebrow, but otherwise didn't move.

Chekov had enjoyed precious little exposure to Vulcans himself, despite four years at Starfleet Academy and three months on board the only human ship in the Fleet with a Vulcan X.O. He'd attended one subspace dynamics lecture by a visiting Vulcan researcher (and followed not a single word of it), and been part of the honor guard that greeted a Vulcan chancellor to San Francisco his freshman year. Other than that, he didn't think he'd even seen Commander Spock in the flesh more than two or three times since setting foot on board the *Enterprise.* Yet despite his admittedly meager experience with the race, there was one thing Chekov understood without question—Vulcans did not like to be touched.

He took a half-step forward to catch the boy's attention, but before he could open his mouth to speak, Spock enfolded the boy's slim hand in his own and delivered a single solemn shake. Eyebrows raised all around the small collection of humans.

"Unfortunately"— the Vulcan released Kirk's hand and took what Chekov suspected was an unconscious step backward —"our time is quite limited, and there are serious matters to which we must attend."

Kirk nodded. "I understand. Ensign Chekov already explained about losing your captain and helmsman."

"I wouldn't say we were lost, exactly." It wasn't the strange black and silver uniform that made Chekov's heart skip a beat, or even the dusting of gray in hair that only a few hours ago had been as black as a midnight sky. It was the easy familiarity with which Sulu smiled at him from where he stood waiting at the back of the group beside Uhura, as though they were both in on some grand joke together and Chekov just didn't realize it yet. "I'd say it's more like we're just seriously misplaced."

* * *

Captain Sulu's presence at least explained why no one at the base camp seemed particularly surprised to meet the younger Kirk.

Chekov tried hard not to stare while he and Tomlinson made their brief report on the search through the karst maze and the location of their not-quite captain. It wasn't easy. Even though he never spoke, Sulu exuded a presence infinitely more commanding than Chekov remembered from their brief meeting a few hours before—a few decades before. He stood at the back of the group and seemed to draw in attention the way a black hole drew in light. And every time Chekov let his gaze stray toward the older man, Sulu was watching him. Not staring, necessarily, but just looking at him, or through him, as though seeing someone else there in his stead. The silent attention made Chekov uneasy.

When Spock finally said, "Thank you, gentlemen," Chekov caught Smith's elbow to hurry her away with him. He was ready to be away from this uncomfortable encounter, someplace private where he could ponder the implications of an older Sulu and a younger Kirk without having to worry about what either of them were thinking of him.

Instead, Spock's impassive voice snared him with a simple, "Mr. Chekov, if you would come with us, please."

Smith bared her teeth in a playful grimace. "Uh-oh," she whispered. "What did you do?"

"I have no idea."

Nor did he find out any time soon. Spock led McCoy and Uhura into the tent they'd been using as a mess hall, apparently trusting that Sulu, Kirk, and Chekov would follow behind. Once there, someone dug rations and water out of an already opened box, and they all found seats on the various tables, chairs, and packages crowded into the shelter. Chekov left his dry rations with Kirk after he saw that the boy had already polished off the two packs he'd been given. He could always find something to eat later, and right now all he wanted to do was sit down.

As soon as he was off his feet, fatigue all but ambushed him, leaving him feeling sick and a little dizzy. He calculated quickly that it had been nearly thirty hours since he'd last slept, and more than half that since he'd had anything to eat. He suddenly felt very stupid for having left his food with Kirk. It helped a little to see that the boy had already finished Chekov's share and was starting in on Uhura's. He tried to remember what it was like to have that sort of bottomless appetite.

When Sulu and Spock had finished explaining the dismal details of Sulu's future, Kirk played with an empty ration packet for another minute or two, folding and unfolding it thoughtfully. He looked neither puzzled nor worried, just pensive. "So you don't remember me as your commander because this alien transporter took me out of your timeline before I became a captain." He shifted a questioning frown to

Spock. "Doesn't that mean you already know I won't be going back?"

"No." Even though he didn't say "captain," Chekov could almost hear the gap where Spock meant the word to fall. "Captain Sulu's future is but one possible future, selected for by your disappearance. If we return you to your own time, we have every reason to believe that the timeline will correct itself to its original course."

Kirk nodded slowly. Folding. Unfolding. "And that's because we have this...bubble to work inside. This time bubble you guys created when you cold-mixed the engines."

"A bubble," McCoy said, "which apparently bursts on 1707."

"So how do we return me to my own time?"

"By figuring out how you—and me—were brought here in the first place." Sulu steadied himself with his good left hand as he took a seat atop one of the tables and folded his legs to lean on. "What were you doing right before you found yourself here?"

Kirk recoiled a little from the intensity of Sulu's gaze. Not in fear, but in the way young men sometimes did from adults they weren't yet sure they trusted. "Riding a shuttle." But he shrugged with a stiff defiance all out of proportion with the question being asked.

"That's it?" McCoy raised his eyebrows in what might have been surprise, glanced at Spock and Uhura, then back at the boy again. "Just riding a shuttle?"

Again the irritated, uncommunicative shrug. "My dad was stationed at a Federation embassy off-world. We were leaving, on our way home." He wadded the ration pack into a ball and flicked it away from him. "There's nothing else to say."

The doctor settled back in his chair and sighed up at Sulu. "Not a lot of points of similarity there."

Sulu's eyes still hadn't left the boy's face. Whatever he saw there made him shake his head slowly. "There has to be something the transporter system keys onto. It can't just be pulling us out randomly."

"Why not?" Kirk crossed his arms and lifted his chin, daring the captain to contradict him. "It's alien, isn't it? Who knows what it thinks is important. Maybe it's what we had for lunch, or the phases of the moon."

"Perhaps." Spock shut the tricorder in his lap and folded his hands atop it. Chekov couldn't tell if the Vulcan simply chose to ignore Kirk's sarcasm, or if he really didn't hear it. "But before making any such assumptions regarding the device's motives, we should acquire more data."

McCoy gave a distinctly unhappy snort. "How? You want to just send someone else into the cave and see who it spits out in exchange?"

"I do not believe that will be necessary, Doctor." Dark eyes locked on Chekov at the other end of the tent, as emotionless and unyielding as a tractor beam. The young ensign suddenly felt himself jolt completely awake and alert. "Mr. Chekov, you have also passed through the alien transporter device, correct?"

"Yes, sir." He tried to sit up a little straighter, only to discover that the morning's cross-country hike in Starfleet issue boots had left him stiff and inflexible. "But it didn't work, sir," he went on, climbing awkwardly to his feet so that he could at least be standing at attention. "I mean, I'm still me, sir—I didn't go anywhere." It was only then that he realized everyone in the tent was staring at him as though he'd just risen from the grave. A cold little knot of fear wound together in his stomach. "Did I?"

"Hey, look on the bright side. At least you're not an Andorian camel anymore."

Uhura glanced across a supply tent that had been hastily cleared and converted into a medical research laboratory through the addition of a portable medical diagnostic bed and a few strong photon lamps. Spock and McCoy were discussing the best way to recalibrate the doctor's medical tricorder now that its sensors were no longer being disrupted by subspace interference from the underground alien transporter. Between them, a very embarrassed-looking Chekov sat hunched on the equipment crate they'd used as a support for the rolled-out diagnostic bed, shirtless and with old-fashioned patch sensors attached to his bare chest and shoulders. Diana Wright was monitoring the readout on her own medical tricorder, and clearly trying to make the shy young ensign feel a little better about being the center of everyone's attention. Even from across the tent, Uhura could see how fast and tense the young Russian's heart rate looked on Wright's display screen.

"Why should it think he was any species of camel?" Sulu asked curiously. After their mud-drenched journey back out of the Tlaoli caves, the older man had gladly exchanged his camouflage jacket and black tunic for a regulation uniform from the original survey team's stores. A mild painkiller injected into his amputated wrist and a cup of steaming coffee had erased a surprising number of the creases from his middle-aged face, but there was still an authoritative note in his voice that made it impossible to mistake him for his younger self. Uhura had noticed that most of the younger officers in the base camp had slipped into the habit of referring to him as "Captain Sulu" without even noticing they were doing it. Even Spock tacked on an occasional "sir," when addressing comments to him, although the older man had never made an issue of it.

Diana Wright cleared her throat a little self-consciously. "When we were down in the cave and all our instruments were malfunctioning, that's what my tricorder thought we were. It was just a joke, sir, to try and get Mr. Chekov to relax. I need a good baseline pulse rate to compare with his old medical records."

"Oh." Sulu paused, eyeing the young Russian with a reminiscent smile. "Pavel, relax. This can't be any worse than that hockey game you played in Murmansk your senior year, when the coach sent you to the showers early and you found out after you were wet that you'd entered the women's locker room by mistake."

Chekov cast him a startled glance and the white line on Wright's display leaped upward for a moment before resuming its rapid pulsing.

"That didn't help," said Wright.

"Sorry." The comment seemed addressed as much to Chekov as to the medic. "I keep forgetting it's only 2266 and you don't really know me yet."

"No, sir." The young ensign looked away, then back again with a little more color in his face. "And it was Minsk."

Sulu lifted an eyebrow. "Are you sure? I thought the national hockey play-offs in 2260 were in Murmansk."

"Minsk," Chekov said again, more strongly. "I made the play-offs both years, '59 and '60. And it was the play-offs in Minsk where I sprained my knee and was sent to the showers early."

"Was that the year you played the team from the Kola Peninsula?"

"No, that was '60. I stayed in that game until the end—"

"Got it," said Wright in satisfaction. "All right, Ensign. You can take your beauty patches off now."

Chekov began to peel off the thin-film sensors, but paused to give the older man across the tent another startled glance. "You did that on purpose."

"Did what?" Sulu asked innocently. "You don't expect an old man like me to remember your high school hockey record perfectly, do you?"

The Russian opened his mouth to reply, then suddenly seemed to remember that the man teasing him was a much higher-ranking officer. Another wave of color mounted his cheeks, then ebbed away again. "No, sir," he said stiffly and finished detaching the rest of Wright's sensors. "Can I leave now?" he asked her.

"We're just getting started, son." McCoy came over to the diagnostic bed with his medical tricorder once again emitting its usual quiet hum. "Put your shirt on, then lie down there again. How were his vitals?" he asked Wright.

"Normal, once he calmed down. And a perfect match for the baseline records we downloaded from the ship. No sign of metabolic aging or change."

McCoy grunted. "That just means he's within a few months of the age he was when he stepped into the machine. Let's try a scan of cellular telomere length." He programmed the tricorder with a few expert flicks of his hand, then swept it across Chekov's stiff, supine form. "Hmm. No statistical difference there, either."

Spock craned his head to peer at the results on the doctor's display screen. "If it exists, the time difference must be of less than one day's duration, or you would see at least a degree of genetic decay. I would suggest scanning for carbon 14 isotopic rations. Mr. Chekov, have you eaten since you came out of the Tlaoli caverns, or drunk anything besides water?"

"No, sir." Even from where he lay on his back, Chekov slipped Uhura a quick, apologetic glance. "I know I was supposed to, sir, but I just didn't feel like it. I made sure to stay hydrated, though."

"Excellent," said the Vulcan, without a trace of concern for the long hours which the young officer had gone without eating. "Your carbon isotopic ratio will not be contaminated by anything except minor atmospheric carbon dioxide, which has equilibrated within your lung tissues."

McCoy frowned as he made adjustments to his medical tricorder. "I'm still not sure how much this is going to tell us, Spock. Even if I compare his C-14 and C-12 ratios to his last baseline exam, there are thousands of things that could have affected them between now and then—"

"But we have a much more recent record of Ensign Chekov's isotopic composition than his last physical, Doctor," said Spock imperturbably. "Unlike you, he was transported down to this planet. Since that was approximately twenty hours ago, his records are still stored in the transporter console's transient buffer."

Diana Wright had stepped back beside Uhura and Sulu to clear more room for McCoy and Spock near the diagnostic bed. "Does the transporter really keep track of things like the individual *isotopes* of carbon in our bodies?" Uhura asked the medic softly as McCoy began a slower scan across Chekov's rigid body. Wright shrugged, but Spock's Vulcan ears must have caught the murmured question. He glanced up from consulting his own scientific tricorder.

"The transporter duplicates our bodies atom for

atom, Lieutenant. That includes discriminating between the light and heavy isotopes of every element which can be fractionated by the body—"

McCoy snorted. "Next you'll be claiming that it keeps track of the quantum spin states in our electron shells. Or the picowatts of electrical discharge along our nerves. Spock, I just don't believe any computer designed by organic beings can process all that information!"

"Indeed." The Vulcan gazed down at the doctor with a familiar air of patient superiority. "Then the isotopic ratios which I have just transmitted from my tricorder to yours must be figments of both our imaginations."

"Hmmph." McCoy examined his tricorder with a scowl, as if it had somehow betrayed him by accepting the data. "All right, let's see how it compares to what I just collected...huh. Well, I'll be a monkey's uncle."

Chekov lifted his head from the diagnostic bed in alarm. "What does it say?"

"Don't worry, there's nothing wrong with you," McCoy assured him. "The isotopic ratios are very close, but they're not identical."

"Nor should they be," pointed out Spock. "Considering the rate at which carbon 14 decays to nitrogen even within human cells. If Doctor McCoy would be kind enough to transfer the isotopic data he has just collected back to my tricorder, I shall extrapolate the decay rate and determine if—" The Vulcan science officer's tricorder beeped and he bent over it immediately. After a moment, he raised his head and gave McCoy a look of reluctant admiration. "I see you have already calibrated your data for decay changes, Doctor. And it appears you are correct. There is indeed a slight discrepancy."

"About five hours, would you say?"

"Five point two five, to be precise."

Chekov pushed himself up to his elbows, his gaze growing more worried as it swung back and forth between the two scientists. "What does that mean?"

"It means," McCoy said, "that you're about five hours younger than you should be."

Silence descended on the supply tent, profound enough that in the distance they could hear the sound of dishes clattering in the mess tent and Sanner's voice from somewhere on one of the nearby karst mounds, calling, "—now dig your crampon into that crack over there to your right—"

"So the alien transporter really did move him through time?" Uhura asked. "Just not as far through time as it moved Captain Kirk and Mr. Sulu?"

"Precisely." Spock stepped back without taking his eyes from the young Russian ensign as McCoy put a hand under Chekov's elbow and helped swing him to his feet. "Now the question we must answer is— why? Ensign, tell me everything you remember about your encounter with the alien force field."

"I can't do that, sir." Chekov met Spock's gaze steadily, although his voice wavered a little with uncertainty. "I don't remember anything about it."

"What do you remember about the time before and after?"

Chekov straightened his shoulders, standing in a posture Uhura recognized as the one you assumed at Starfleet Academy when you were being quizzed at the end of a field exercise. "I remember falling down from the ledge we were walking to get into the cave, sir. The next thing I remember after that is waking up in the dark. After a while, Lieutenant Uhura and the other cave team members came and found me there. They told me that Captain Kirk and I disappeared together, but I don't remember any of it."

"Fascinating." Spock turned his probing gaze from Chekov to Uhura, and she could see the young man's shoulders slump a little in relief. "Lieutenant, after Ensign Chekov fell from that ledge, he remained with your rescue party?"

"Yes, sir." Something was niggling at the back of her mind, but Spock's lifted eyebrows told her he was waiting for additional information. "He came with us from the waterfall where he fell, to the cave where we found the lost survey team. We waited there to see if the ship could beam us out, then we tried to walk out of the cave again. Ensign Chekov was with us the whole time, mapping our path back down the main alien conduit to the ice cave where we encountered the alien force field for the first time. Then he and Captain Kirk vanished together."

Spock nodded. "How many hours would you estimate that took?"

"About three?" Uhura glanced instinctively at Chekov for confirmation and saw him wince. Regretting her own lack of memory, she turned to look at Wright instead. "Did you notice?"

"My chronometer wasn't working, but I'd guess it was closer to three and a half," the medic said.

"That would fit with ship records of your communications from the cave," Spock agreed. "After the ensign vanished, how long did it take until you found him again?"

"About another hour and a half," Uhura said, then belatedly did the math. "Which adds up to five hours."

"Indeed." Spock steepled his fingers and gently rested them against his chin. "If the Ensign Chekov we have here was transported by the alien device through time from the point at which he fell from the ledge to the point at which you found him in the upper cavern of the cave system—"

"The same cavern that you found me being healed in?" Sulu asked shrewdly.

"Yes," Uhura said, and it was more than just an answer to the older man's question. "That would make him five hours younger than he should have been." The memory niggling at the back of her mind suddenly shouldered its way into her consciousness, and she gasped. "When we found Ensign Chekov at the bottom of the waterfall below that ledge—Diana, do you remember how disoriented he seemed? He kept saying that it seemed like things had already happened—"

"And that it seemed as if it had been a long time since he had fallen from the ledge," the medic agreed. "He was fine, physically, except for being wet and hypothermic, but it did seem like it took him a while to get back to normal."

"But I couldn't have gone straight from falling off the ledge to the cave where they found me five hours later," Chekov protested. "If I did, who was with them for the rest of that time?"

"You were," Spock answered calmly. "A version of you taken from another point of time and sent backward to replace yourself."

The young ensign cast Uhura a slightly hunted look, and she stepped forward to stand beside him. "But what point could that version have come from, Mr. Spock?" she asked gently. "He was wearing his caving suit and had all his same tools with him—"

"Except the cave map," Diana Wright reminded her. "We thought he lost that falling down through the water, but maybe he never had it."

"It is likely that he had it the *first* time he fell," Spock said. "If my current hypothesis is correct, that would have been the time when he was drowned by his fall." He held up a hand when Uhura, Wright, and Chekov all tried to speak at once, and they obediently fell silent. "I suspect you managed to revive him on that first time through the events in question. It would therefore have been *that* Mr. Chekov who first encountered the Tlaoli transport device. At the moment the slightly older Mr. Chekov stepped into it, the device sent his healthy body backward in time for you to find beside the waterfall, and sent the younger Mr. Chekov's drowned body forward through time to the cavern with the healing chambers. The same place to which it sent Captain Sulu and young Mr. Kirk when it replaced both of them with their healthier counterparts."

There was another long silence as they absorbed what Spock had said. He glanced around at their startled faces, lifted a quizzical eyebrow, and added, "This is, of course, still merely a hypothesis."

"How can we prove it?" McCoy demanded. "Or disprove it? It's not even a hypothesis, Spock, if there's no way to do that."

The Vulcan science officer gave him an exasperated look. "We will first subject my idea to critical analysis, Doctor. If it remains feasible after that, then we will move on to the next phase of examination."

"Well, I think it makes sense for me to be replaced by a healthier version of myself." Sulu touched the empty right sleeve of his regulation gold tunic. "And if the alien device had no way of knowing that Chekov was going to recover from being drowned, then I suppose it made sense for it to replace him, too. But what about your missing Captain Kirk? That young man I just met looked as fit as a young wolf cub—and about as self-reliant as one, too. Why replace him with an older version?"

"Unless he wasn't telling us the truth about where he came from," McCoy said slowly. "I think I should go talk to him."

The sound of a cleared throat caught everyone's attention, but it took Uhura and the rest of them a minute to realize the unlikely source. Ensign Chekov, who had retreated to the shadows of the supply tent while they discussed the mechanics of the alien time transport system, now stepped back into the fringe of the strong lights. "Sir, if you don't mind, I think maybe I should do that," he suggested tentatively. "I'm not that much older than he is, after all."

Chekov's rationale made Spock look baffled, but McCoy's blue eyes twinkled in comprehension. "That you aren't, son. Why don't you go see what you can do? If young Jim Kirk won't talk to you, just bring him back here and we'll see if I can do any better."

The young Russian nodded and slid out of the supply tent quickly, as if he was afraid they'd drag him back for some last medical test if he delayed. Sulu watched him go with a reminiscent smile. "I'd forgotten what a worrier he was when he was young," he commented to Uhura. "Once you're friends, you need to remind him not to take everything so seriously."

She nodded in agreement, but even as she did, Uhura felt a small shiver of something that was not quite déjà vu and not quite fear. It was unsettling to get these small, slanting glimpses into her own personal future. The larger picture of future wars and galactic disasters that this older Sulu had painted was abstract enough for her to comprehend, even if it was disturbing. It was the tiny, almost unconscious revelations of future friendships and confidences that made the skin prickle on the back of her neck.

"All right, Spock," McCoy was saying. "What else do we need to do to prove whether or not this idea of yours holds water? We have only fifty more hours to get Captain Kirk back, remember."

"Forty-eight point nine hours, to be precise," Spock corrected him. "And once we have resolved the anomalous data point of why the machine would have exchanged our James Kirk for his younger self, the only remaining question is one of intention. We do not know what the aliens who designed this system originally intended it to accomplish. If they meant to permanently replace the individuals whom they exchanged through time, then there may be no way for us to reverse the process. But if they intended the exchange to be temporary, then they must also have designed the transporter to work in both directions. Unfortunately, we cannot know—"

"Maybe we can, Commander," Uhura interrupted. "I didn't have time to tell you before, but we found alien writing down in the system of conduits between the ice cave and the healing chamber. There might be enough there for our translators to decode."

"That would be of great assistance," Spock admitted. "Even so, we will need to go about the next phase of our proceedings with the greatest care and caution."

"Why?" McCoy asked, frowning. "What is this next phase, anyway?"

"The one prescribed by the scientific method for any valid hypothesis," the Vulcan said. "Experimentation."

Chapter Five

THE DRUMMING OF RAIN against the *Drake*'s hull suddenly sounded twice as loud to Sulu, as if his senses had been intensified by shock. He stared at the older man across the shuttle's cockpit, taking in his battle-scarred face, the green and violet camouflage jacket streaked with rain, and the unfamiliar Starfleet insignia, thin and luminous as silver wire, on his black uniform collar.

"You were my navigator twenty years ago?" Sulu repeated, as if hearing it in his own voice could somehow make it more comprehensible. "Aboard the *Enterprise?*"

The older man who'd said he was Pavel Chekov glanced around the shuttle instead of replying. His frown touched only his forehead; his mouth seemed to be held in an unchanging grim line by the network of old scars around it. "Which *Enterprise* shuttle is this? The *Copernicus?* The *Jocelyn Bell?* I remember we lost the *Hawking* studying a supernova...but that might not have happened yet for you."

"It's the *Edwin Drake.*"

"I don't remember that one." Chekov reached out to touch the instrument panel with the kind of nostalgic affection Sulu had once seen Scotty display toward an obsolescent voltmeter he'd found in an emergency tool kit. "What a relic....How the hell did you get here in it?"

"I didn't fly here," Sulu said. "I got transported by some kind of alien force field from Tlaoli 4."

Chekov's gaze came back to Sulu's face and the weather-beaten creases around his eyes deepened, although it was hard to tell if the expression was one of surprise or of suspicion. "I don't remember visiting any planet named Tlaoli, much less losing you there. What year is it for you?"

"It's 2268, stardate 1704.4." Sulu saw the blank look on Chekov's face and tried to think what might have stuck in his memory after twenty years. "Right after I caught the Psi 2000 virus and ran through the ship pretending to be D'Artagnon. You must remember *that.*"

"Actually, I don't." Chekov mulled it over, rubbing a hand absently across one shoulder as if it ached. "I was just out of the academy in 2268—I didn't know any of the senior officers. But I would have remembered if we lost a shuttle." He flicked a glance at

Sulu's face. "The whole ship talked about it when Mr. Spock was stranded on Taurus II with the *Galileo*. We all expected Captain Mitchell to throw Commissioner Ferris into the brig for ordering us to—"

"Captain *who?*"

"Gary Mitchell. Or maybe he was still the ship's first officer when you—" The older Chekov broke off abruptly, as if something in the quality of Sulu's silence had alerted him. "Mitchell isn't your second-in-command," he stated with a perceptiveness that startled Sulu. Had the young Russian ensign he'd met back on Tlaoli possessed the same shrewdness beneath his awkward uncertainty, Sulu wondered, or had his apparently violent future sharpened his wits? "Who is?"

"Our science officer, Mr. Spock," Sulu said. "We lost Mitchell early in our five-year mission, when Captain Kirk tried to take the ship past the edge of the galaxy."

They stared at each other through a swirling gauze of gnats, until the older man finally cursed and flapped a hand across his face. "This is too complicated to figure out here. And it isn't safe to stay. The Gorn have probably sent out automated surface trackers to home in on your warp core's radiation signature. I'm surprised they're not already crawling all over you."

"The warp core and engines are magnetically shielded," Sulu said. "And I'm not sure—"

Chekov had already swung back toward the shuttle's cargo hold, but he paused to throw a sharp look across his shoulder. "You're not sure you trust me." He made it a statement rather than a question, as if it seemed to him a perfectly sensible way to feel. "What you don't know is that you and I are probably the last two humans left alive on Basaraba. This is a Gorn planet, and you've already found out how they treat anyone they don't know." He swept his weapon's gleaming snout around and Sulu instinctively flinched, but all Chekov did was rap on the communicator's power switch and deaden its displays. "Starfleet can't help us anymore. And there's a chance the Klingons might be able to decode a signal as old as that one."

Klingons? Sulu's sense of having fallen into a nightmare dimension deepened abruptly. The feeling was enhanced when Chekov slung his weapon up across his good shoulder and left the cockpit without another word, like a mystical figure in a dream. Whether or not Sulu followed was apparently up to him.

It took Sulu only a few seconds to decide that his best chance of survival in this alien hell lay with someone who had already survived it for a while. And for some reason, he had no doubt that this Pavel Chekov was that person. There was something stubbornly real about the older man, grim and battle-hardened as he was, that defied any attempt to see him as either an alien-induced hallucination or an imposter. With a resolute breath that stirred up swirls of startled gnats, Sulu scrambled to his feet and followed the other man out of the wrecked shuttle.

They paused in the cargo hold long enough to scoop up the emergency food supplies Sulu had packed, but left the water behind. "No shortage of that on Basaraba," Chekov said. "We salvaged a heavy-duty purification unit from the *Hotspur.*"

Sulu hefted his bag of supplies and followed the older man out through the shuttle's half-sprung hatch into the night. To his surprise, the rain was neither as cold nor as driving as he'd expected from the sound of it on the shuttle's hull. Instead, it came down in a way he remembered from an orchid-collecting trip he'd once made to Jamaica, a lukewarm, dripping shower with only an occasional drench as leafy branches far overhead dumped the moisture that had pooled on them. Despite the pleasant warmth and humidity, however, Sulu soon found himself wishing he had on something more waterproof than his uniform tunic. The rain-sodden cloth chafed where the bag of supplies swung back and forth over his shoulder, and plastered so tight to his skin elsewhere that his sweat stayed trapped beneath it.

Despite the rain, or perhaps because of it, the forest was hushed enough for Sulu to hear the rasp of Chekov's breath as he led the way down a vine-draped alley through the trees. "Water buffalo path," the other man said over his shoulder. Then, because it seemed to occur to him that he ought to explain further: "Not really water buffaloes, that's just what we call them. They're about twice as big."

"Dangerous?"

Chekov snorted. "Only if you fall asleep and don't

smell them coming. They move about a kilometer an hour, fertilizing the soil all the way."

Now that he had mentioned it, Sulu could smell the musky organic odor stirred up under his feet. He expanded his mental wish list from rain gear to waterproof hiking boots. The buffalo trail angled uphill, and Sulu could tell from the way his own breath began to rasp in his throat that they were either at high altitude, or on a planet with an atmosphere less dense than Earth's. "You mentioned Klingons," he said, to take his mind off his unsatisfied need for oxygen. "In your time, they're at war with the Federation?"

"They're part of the Gorn Hegemony." Chekov paused a moment, as if trying to think back. "Have you met the Gorn yet?"

"No."

"Nasty reptiles with a huge grudge against the Federation. We had a battle with them a few decades ago and got them exiled from space as a result. They never forgave us. A few years later, they found a way to strike back using a new kind of trans-space portal to send their armies directly from planet to planet. They wiped out and enslaved the Romulans in less than a year. The Klingons signed a war powers pact with them not too long after that." Chekov's voice turned a shade more grim. "The Federation has been fighting them for almost seventeen years now."

"And this is one of their planets?"

"This is the hub of their entire trans-space transport system." Chekov fell silent again, perhaps to let

Sulu absorb the impact of that. "The *Hotspur* ran across it by accident a few weeks ago. We notified the Federation, but we knew it would take them months to organize an invasion that could reach this deep into Gorn space. So once we saw that the hub was a permanent fortress, not something the Gorn could pack up and move—"

"That stone building with the tall towers?"

"Yes. We decided to attack. It looked like the Gorn were massing a large force here, maybe for an invasion of one of our home planets. We were afraid a few months might be too long to wait for reinforcements."

Sulu nodded, but had to wait a moment to speak. The trail was getting steeper, but despite his own ragged breath, Chekov didn't seem to see any need to moderate his pace. "How did it go, the attack?"

Even in the darkness, he could sense irritation in the glance Chekov threw him, as if the question had been not only pointless but also remarkably stupid. "When I told you we were the last two humans on Basaraba, what did you think that meant?" the older man asked sarcastically. "That everyone else on the *Hotspur* had gone away for a week of R and R?"

"No, I assumed they were all dead," Sulu said as evenly as he could manage between gasps. "But even a suicide attack can be a tactical success."

"Well, ours wasn't." And that was the end of the conversation.

The buffalo trail angled up a forested ridge at a

surprising slant for a path carved by such large herbi-
vores. Sulu could feel the muscles in his legs burn as
his lungs struggled in vain to pull more oxygen out of
the thin air. The towering trees into which he had
crashed the *Drake* had been left behind as the rain
drifted into a thick and clinging fog. The higher they
climbed, the more the trees shrank, until Sulu found
himself walking through a shoulder-high cloud forest
whose shrubs were webbed with flowering epiphytes
and hanging streamers of violet moss.

Along the jagged crest of the ridge, even the
shrubs thinned out in places to barren scars of talus
and stone. Chekov turned off the buffalo trail and
headed for the nearest of those clearings. Sulu followed him, so intent on keeping pace despite his
aching lungs that he barely noticed when the other
man came to a sudden halt. Chekov threw out a ward-
ing hand, but it was too late. Sulu had already run
into what felt like a curving wall of solid metal, even
though all he saw ahead of him was air.

"I probably should have mentioned that I left the
cloaking device on." Although Chekov didn't sound
particularly remorseful about his omission.

Sulu stepped back, rubbing at the sore spot on his
forehead, which had taken the brunt of the unexpected impact. "It wouldn't have mattered, since I
wouldn't know a cloaking device if it hit me. Which,"
he added dryly, "it apparently just did."

"It didn't hit you, *you* hit it." Chekov was tapping
some kind of code into a small hand-held device.

"And technically, it wasn't the cloaking device you hit. It was the shuttle."

Sulu opened his mouth to say something in reply, but a sudden metallic ripple in the air above him made him curse and duck away involuntarily. A parabolic wing materialized so close overhead that it seemed as if he should have somehow sensed its presence, followed by a familiar blunt-nosed fuselage with a darkened cockpit window. With an involuntary shudder that made his sweaty uniform tunic feel clammy and cold, Sulu recognized one of the alien fighters that had chased him.

"It's a Gorn ship," Chekov said, once again reading Sulu's silent reaction with unexpected shrewdness. "Equipped with a Romulan-designed cloaking device to make it invisible, just like all the others. We sacrificed the *Hotspur* to bring it down, so we could use it to infiltrate Tesseract Fortress with our last pulse bombs."

Sulu frowned, remembering the violent explosion he had materialized into. "I think maybe I saw that attack."

"I *know* you did," the older man retorted. "It's the only reason I'm still alive. The Gorn assumed your shuttle was the attack ship. If they'd realized it was one of their own cloaked fighters, they could easily have brought me down by cross-firing their energy disruptors." He clambered up onto one wing and levered open the opaque cockpit window, then swung himself down into the interior and promptly vanished. "It tells you everything you need to know about the Gorn that they don't bother to make their own ships immune to their weapons," said his muffled voice from inside. "And that they don't believe in sitting down when they fly. Can you make it in?"

"I think so." Despite his younger muscles, it still took Sulu two tries to haul himself up the slippery polymer surface of the fighter's sleek wing. He finally wriggled up on his belly far enough to clamp his fingers around the edge of the open hatch, then hung gasping there for a moment, peering down inside. The aura of dreamlike unreality that kept washing over him on this planet came flooding in stronger than ever when he saw the Gorn cockpit. Chekov sat on a bare metal floor, strapping blocks of wood to his muddy boots so he could reach the controls, which were arranged in a half-circle high under the translucent cockpit window. There was no rudder, no screens or instrument gauges, only a few rows of switches and several indented hollows that must be hand-activated flight or weapons controls.

"Get in," said the older man. "There's plenty of room—the Gorn are a lot bigger than we are." He stood, balancing himself on his makeshift stilts with surprising ease. "Wedge yourself in or you'll get a close-up view of the warp core when we accelerate. The Gorn also don't bother to insulate their cockpits from their engine compartments."

"How nice." Sulu heaved himself over the rim and dropped several feet down to an unpadded metal floor. "It doesn't look like they bother to soundproof either."

Chekov fished the cockpit cover closed with a long branch, then pulled on a black helmet marked with the same wire-thin Starfleet insignia that he wore on his uniform collar. "There are more of our helmets in back. They generate sound-damping fields, but there's nothing they can do about the subsonic reverb."

Sulu hunted around until he found the helmets Chekov had mentioned, wedged against a strut support near the Gorn shuttle's left wing. One was a little too small for him, but the other fit perfectly—so perfectly, in fact, that it felt as if it were made for him. Sulu was suddenly reminded that when Chekov had first responded to his anonymous distress signal, he had called for him by name. And by title.

"This ship, the *Hotspur,* that you came here on—" he began, but Chekov was already flipping switches. The Gorn shuttle's engines coughed to life behind him, wobbling up to an unbalanced and deafening roar before the helmet's sound-dampening fields threw a muffled veil of artificial silence over the noise. Sulu cleared his throat and was startled to find he couldn't hear that sound, either. He guessed that advanced communicator technology had learned to distinguish voices from other sounds. "Chekov?"

"Yes?" The Russian-accented voice somehow sounded more familiar when it was separated from the older man's scarred presence, as if it could still belong to that diffident young ensign back on Tlaoli.

"The ship you came here on as second-in-command, the *Hotspur*—" Sulu said again. "Who was her captain?"

The silence that followed his question vibrated

with more than just the silent subsonic reverberations of the Gorn shuttle's roar. "You were," Chekov said brusquely. "Until you died today in Tesseract Fortress."

"That's it! Just kick off and fall—you've got a good ten meters!"

Sanner's voice drifted cheerfully over the sunny plain, as unaffected and natural as if it were the song of some native bird. Chekov envied his easy nature. The geologist stood at the foot of one of the towering karst erratics with his head tipped back and his weight thrown into the rope he had looped around behind him. Above him, Kirk dangled on the other end of the line, effortlessly rappelling himself down the rock face in long, lazy arcs. They might have been a father and son on vacation, instead of a quirky Starfleet geologist and a temporally displaced civilian boy.

Sanner grinned at Chekov as he drew near. "Hey, Ensign! Want to give it a try?"

Even without the hours underground and the long morning of hiking, the suggestion would have made his stomach curl. "I've already had enough climbing on rocks for this mission, sir." But he added, "Thank you," anyway, so that Sanner wouldn't be offended.

The geologist laughed so heartily that Chekov suspected he'd asked only because he'd thought the reaction would be worth it. Hopping to one side, Sanner made room for Kirk as the boy dropped the last few meters to the ground. "Too bad we didn't have Jim here when we were making that stupid human pyramid." He tossed aside the rope only to catch the pair of gloves Kirk underhanded in his direction. "He's a natural."

"I did a little rock climbing before." Kirk tried to sound casual as he unbuckled the leather harness, but Chekov recognized that faint redness in his cheeks. He felt the same thrill of embarrassed pleasure every time a commanding officer complimented him, however slightly. "Me and my brother went to Yosemite on an Outward Bound trip a couple of years ago."

"Next time you go," Sanner told him, "hit some of the really big South American caves. You'll give all your rock climbing gear a good workout, and get to see some great flowstone to boot."

"Sounds great." Kirk let the harness drop to the ground, then used one foot to kick it up into his hands as though totally unaware of the strength and athleticism involved in the movement. Maybe he was. "Thanks, Zap."

Sanner accepted the gear with a smile. "Pleasure's all mine." Then he cocked a nod toward Chekov as he stooped to begin pulling in the rope. "I'll take care of this stuff. You go on with Mr. Chekov." Another puckish grin made his eyes twinkle. "Next time, I'll take you *under*ground."

Chekov waited until they were out of Sanner's earshot to comment, "I should have come with you. It looks like you had more fun."

Kirk wrinkled his nose as he swiped at the dust on

the knees of his pants. "That science stuff can get so boring. I'd rather be doing something." He straightened. "So—did they figure out if you were your own evil twin?"

Chekov nodded. "I was apparently switched for another version of myself, just like you and Mr. Sulu." He couldn't believe he said it so calmly. The chill that had set in when Spock first declared him five hours too young hadn't faded. In fact, he felt like he'd been dunked in frigid water, and wondered if he'd ever be warm again. "It's strange," he said, after what seemed a very long time. "I don't feel any different—I don't feel like I'm not *me*. But I almost drowned yesterday when we first came down to the planet, and now Mr. Spock tells me that I probably *did* drown in some parallel timeline. I wouldn't be here right now if the alien transporter hadn't shifted me by a few hours...." He stole a glance at Kirk, then looked away again when he found the boy's expression self-consciously blank and unreadable. "Maybe it's easier to accept when the gap between then and now is bigger."

Kirk didn't look up from where he kicked a rock ahead of him as they walked. "It isn't." He didn't say anything for a time, then asked, with that same studious neutrality, "Are they going to make you go back?"

The question wasn't what Chekov had expected. "I don't know," he admitted, oddly bothered by the thought. "The device only moved me a few hours, so it's hard to tell how much impact—if any—it had on the timeline."

"But if they found out it had some big impact? Like—" The boy lifted one shoulder in an awkward shrug, his brows knitting with frustration as he struggled to express what he was thinking. "Like some other guy was supposed to get your job after you died, and he went on to be some important admiral who did all kinds of important things. Would they make you go back then?"

"I…" Chekov clenched his jaw on the facile answer that wanted to spring out of him. *No, of course they wouldn't send me back. I'm a part of this crew—I'm allowed to be here.* But if Spock was right, he was really part of some other crew, some other timeline, with no more right to continue than Kirk or Captain Sulu. The fact that he couldn't remember the details of his removal didn't grant him any special dispensation. In the end, all he could say was, "I don't know. I'd like to think that I would do what was right for everyone involved, but I really don't know."

"Even if you knew you were just going back there to die?"

Something in the boy's tone made Chekov pull him to a stop and face him. "No one's going to send you back in time just to die. It's because our timeline says that you lived and became a successful starship commander that we're trying to figure out how to send you back at all."

Kirk lifted stark eyes to the young Russian's face. "Then maybe I didn't come from your timeline."

Chekov let go of his arm, but didn't step away. "What was happening before you came here?" He tried to make the question sound casual, but couldn't ignore the fear stirring behind the boy's fierce expression. Troubled waters beneath a fragile, icy surface.

"I was riding in a shuttle..."

Chekov nodded. "That's what you said before."

"No—" Kirk cut him off impatiently, pressing on as though afraid of what would happen if he stopped. "I mean I was riding in a shuttle full of security commandos." He looked to one side and heaved a deep, steadying breath. This time, Chekov didn't interrupt. "For the last nine months or so, my dad's been stationed at the embassy on Grex." He gave Chekov permission to speak by flicking a glance in his direction. "Do you know about Grex?"

He didn't know if the name referred to a planet or a government or a space station. Whichever it was, Chekov didn't recognize it, so he only shook his head and let Kirk continue.

"They're kind of midrange on the Richter Scale of Cultures." Having something to explain seemed to calm Kirk a little, steady him. *I'd rather be doing something,* he'd told Chekov earlier. "Like they use hydrocarbon fuels and they use radio and stuff, but they never went atomic. Anyway, for a long time they were an Orion slave republic."

"They had extensive unmined dilithium deposits?"

Chekov guessed. It wouldn't have been the first time the Orions took advantage of a less advanced civilization. They were thieves more than villains, basically shrugging off whatever primitive defenses the locals could muster as they stripped the planet of any resources they found desirable. Every now and then they would actually interact with the natives and make them into an Orion version of a "republic." More often, though, they left as inexplicably as they had arrived, leaving a barren, shell-shocked population behind them.

"This time it was just their location," Kirk said. "The Orions were using the planet as a waypoint for their pirating fleet. You know—storage, refueling, R and R." He started walking again, but more slowly this time, as though picking his way through dangerous territory. "The Federation wouldn't do anything about it, because Grex isn't a Federation member, and the Orions are their own government, and we can't go sticking our noses into their business all the time." Chekov thought he heard echoes of someone else's voice in the boy's bitter commentary. "So at some point, the Grexxan natives got hold of an Orion subspace transmitter and called the Federation for help." He gave a surprisingly cynical snort. "I guess we can butt into the Orions' business as long as somebody else asks us."

"How did you get there?" Chekov asked.

"My dad was with the peacekeeping force that chased off the Orions. He stayed to run security for the embassy. About a year in, he figured it was safe enough to bring me and my mom and brother out to stay with him for a while."

He fell abruptly silent. Chekov waited while they passed into the shadow of another tall karst column and the dry Tlaoli breeze chased little brush tangles across their path. By then, the silence had stretched too long and hard and painful to endure. "It wasn't safe, though," Chekov finally ventured. "Was it?"

Kirk didn't answer right away, and Chekov thought for a moment that he'd breached the line he'd promised himself he wouldn't cross—he'd treated Kirk like a child, and wrested away control of the conversation like every other impatient adult. But instead of pulling away, the boy only shook his head slowly and sank back to lean on the wall of stone. "One of the native groups got a bunch of weapons out of the stashes the Orions left behind." His voice was steadier now, almost without emotion. "I don't know their names, or what they're fighting about, or any of the political stuff that's going on. But I guess the Orions kept them from fighting with each other for thirty or forty years, and now that the Orions are gone they want to pick up where they left off." His hands, trembling like small, frightened animals, crept into his pockets of their own volition, without his even glancing down. "They started shooting each other in the streets, and shooting the Federation personnel. They had maybe half the city torn up, then they started in on the embassy. My dad and his men were shoving us onto transports just to get us off the ground. There's a ship, the *Eliza Mae,* that's supposed to show up for a supply run in another day or so. We figured we could all stay in orbit, where we ought to be safe, and wait for her." He swallowed hard, like he was swallowing a rock. "I was on a ship with a bunch of the security guys. They shot us down while we were still over the city—I don't know how, they're not supposed to have anything that can do that. But they breached the shuttle as soon as we touched down, and Lieutenant Maione told me to get out and run." The first sparkle of tears pooled in his eyes. "I should have stayed with them."

Chekov didn't have to ask what had happened to the security squad. "You couldn't have done anything."

"I should have stayed with them," he insisted fiercely. "You're not supposed to just leave people who are fighting for you! You're not supposed to leave them behind!"

"It was their job to protect you. They would rather you were away and safe."

"Only I'm not! I wasn't! I didn't know which way to go, and there was so much fighting back toward the embassy. I tried to find my dad, but they caught me! They caught me before I even got ten blocks, and they…"

He dragged the back of his hand across his eyes, but even the sleeves of his neat civilian tunic couldn't catch the tears suddenly spilling over onto his cheeks.

He bit his lip to keep from sobbing, then bent almost double to hide his face in his hands.

Chekov recognized that fear only too well, understood how it could strip you naked without warning and leave you feeling weak and helpless even after you were hours and hours away. "They killed you." Just to say it, he had to swallow down the knot of nausea that had suddenly curdled in the pit of his stomach.

The boy dropped his hands away from his face, but didn't straighten. "He had the rifle right in my face. I could see blood on the barrel where he'd shot other people, and it smelled like oil and burned sulfur...." When he finally looked up, the pain on his face was so naked, Chekov had to blink back his own tears of sympathy. "That's where this machine sent your captain." Remorse and fear and confusion braided his voice into an agony. "I know he's great and all, and he's supposed to get the whole universe out of trouble, and I'm sorry I ran away from the shuttle and put everybody in this mess—but I don't see how he could have got out of that. This machine sent him back there and killed him." He reached across and seized Chekov's wrist like a lifeline. "And if you sent me back, it's just going to kill me, too."

Chapter Six

THE PORTAL YAWNED before them, dim and shadowy with mist. Cold silence seemed to flow out of it, stealing away the small sounds of breath and movement that would normally have accompanied the eight-person research team that stood on its rocky threshold.

"My tricorder detects no trace of subspace activity." Spock's voice sounded deeper and more somber than usual as it broke the hush. It was midafternoon, and Tlaoli's karstlands lay windless and still under the ephemeral heat of its pale sun. "I believe it will be safe to go in through this opening."

"As long as you don't mind coming out somewhere halfway across the galaxy," muttered the irrepressible Zap Sanner to archaeologist Carolyn Palamas, who was shifting nervously beside him.

Uhura gave the cave expert a repressive look. Fortunately, Spock was already moving into the shadow of the main cavern entrance and didn't notice Sanner's sarcastic comment. Palamas, however, looked even more anxious than she had before.

Uhura took a deep breath in a vain attempt to quiet her own unease, then followed the Vulcan science officer into the natural cave opening. The half-domed chamber that lay beyond the rock portal looked exactly the same now as it had twenty-four hours ago when she'd followed Captain James T. Kirk into it. Dry limestone walls, a scattering of fallen flowstone shards, a few faint fingers of mist rising from the places where the cave floor had dissolved down through to the cavern's lower level—it all looked very ordinary, as if nothing more dangerous lay beyond this chamber than a few tight cave squeezes and a narrow ledge or two. Uhura tried to recall how she had felt, coming in that very first time, but her memories were too strongly colored by the hours she'd spent after that, trapped in the darkness and cold. She reached up to thumb the igniter on her carbide helmet light, and found its downward wash of light oddly reassuring.

"Subspace activity still below detection limits," announced Spock's imperturbable voice from the darkness ahead of her. He hadn't yet turned on his own helmet lamp, but he moved with surprising confidence toward the nearest misty floor well.

"Watch where you're going, Spock," McCoy called from beside Uhura. "Jaeger said some of those holes go straight down to the cave where they found that alien force field."

"Precisely why I wish to record the subspace emissions coming through them, Doctor." Spock crouched on the lip of one open shaft and swung his bulky tricorder out into its rising plume of mist. Uhura tried to notice if the instrument caught an upward reflection of blue alien light, but all she saw were the spiky shadows she and McCoy threw across the floor as more people entered and lit carbide lights behind them. "Subspace readings appear minimal, consistent with the alien transporter having returned to low-power status."

"It could also be consistent with your tricorder starting to malfunction." Sulu crossed the cave to join the much taller Vulcan. Suited up in a neat cave jumpsuit and helmet, with his carbide light throwing concealing shadows across his lined face, the former starship captain looked remarkably like his younger self. When he spoke, however, the crisp certainty in his voice marked him as an officer long used to being in command. Spock silently acknowledged both the comment and the authority by running a systems check on his instrument.

"Internal readings show very low error levels," he said. "The magnetic shielding that I had Mr. Scott construct for our instruments appears to block out both the power-draining and subspace interference effects, just as it did for our shuttles. I believe we may proceed with caution into the cave's lower level."

Uhura glanced back at the cave entrance, where a

handful of glittering carbide lights drowned out the pale glow of Tlaoli sunlight. Of the original survey party that had been trapped down here, only security guard Yuki Smith and archaeologist Carolyn Palamas had been pronounced sufficiently recovered from their ordeal to be included in this third foray into the cavern. Chekov had once again been drafted to help Smith carry their research equipment, and Sulu had insisted on joining the team, as well. Unlike young Kirk—who had been just as eager to come with them—the former starship captain had wielded enough clout to override Spock's reluctance.

"Ready, Mr. Sanner?" Uhura asked.

"Almost." The cave specialist was already stationed beside one of the larger pits in the floor, fishing a knotted rope and pitons from his equipment bag with his usual energy and enthusiasm. "I'm going to turn my carbide off once I climb down there," he said, as he hammered several pitons into the floor and knotted the rope securely around them. "I'd appreciate you guys not shining your lights down to watch me. If that force field is active, I want to have a chance to see it before it sees me."

"The human eye," Spock said, "can detect a single photon of light once it has adapted to the dark. It is one of the few physiological capabilities at which humans excel."

"Uh...thanks, Commander." Sanner tugged at the rope to test it, then swung himself out into the open shaft that plunged down through the thick cave floor.

The glow of his light descended a few meters, then winked out abruptly. "Well, it sure seems dark down here," said his echoing voice from below.

"Wait a bit to make sure your eyes have adjusted," McCoy advised. There was a long pause, then the rope wriggled against its pitons as Sanner clambered farther down it. "Still pretty dark," he said after another moment. "And a little cold, but nothing like it was the last time we were—ouch!"

Uhura restrained herself with difficulty from leaning over to look for him. "What's the matter, Zap?"

"I climbed down into one of those damned flowstone pillars that formed beneath the solution pits up there. And now the rope's all tangled in it....I'm going to have to burn some carbide after all, or I'll never make it down to the floor." A pause, a series of clicks, then Sanner called in a completely different voice, "Hey! Lieutenant, I think I can see some of that writing you wanted us to look for."

Uhura braced herself at the edge of the open shaft with her own carbide angled down into the mist. "On the pillar?"

"No, on the side of the cave." The rope moved a little more strongly, and she could see the diffuse glow of Sanner's carbide light swing back and forth like a pendulum through the dark. It looked like he was scanning his carbide glow along as much of the cave wall as he could reach. "I don't think this is a cave at all! Now that the ice has melted off, you can see that the walls are made of that same purple metal as the conduits we were in before. And those little ant-track marks are *everywhere*."

Sulu's intent gaze met Uhura's through the rising plume of mist. Along with Spock and McCoy, he had come to crouch on the verge of the solution pit to watch Sanner below. "It could be an instruction manual for using the time transporter."

Spock lifted an ambivalent eyebrow. "Possibly, Captain. However it is just as likely to be a listing of allowable baggage limits for travelers."

"Or an advertisement for a prehistoric tourist resort," added McCoy dryly.

The rope jerked and shifted a few more times, then abruptly went slack. "Sanner?" Uhura called down the shaft.

"Don't worry, I'm still here, Lieutenant." She could see the glow of his carbide brighten in the swirling fog in the former ice cave as he glanced up toward them. "I'm on the floor now, and I'm going to turn off my carbide again. Tell everyone up there to look away. From *all* the holes," he added emphatically.

Uhura backed away from the opening in the floor, then glanced over her shoulder in time to see Chekov tug Smith away from another of the open solution holes. Sulu, McCoy, and Spock stepped away, too, turning so that their carbide lights were angled back toward the pale glow of daylight outside. There was a long, anxious silence.

"I think I see a little bit of blue force field," Sanner's muffled voice said at last. "But it seems to be confined to the top of one large flowstone mound right in the middle of the cave."

"You think that might be an alien field generator covered in a flowstone shell, like those healing chambers we saw back at the other end of the cave?" McCoy asked.

"Quite possibly, Doctor." Spock swung his shielded tricorder up across one shoulder as he prepared to follow Sanner. "I will give you a more definitive answer once I have measured its subspace emissions. Lieutenant Uhura, you and Lieutenant Palamas may descend and begin translating the alien script as soon as I have established a safety perimeter."

Uhura nodded and saw Carolyn Palamas take a reluctant step forward with her own shielded equipment, a dedicated archaeological translator with visual scanning capabilities. "And the rest of the party?"

Spock glanced across at Smith and Chekov, who had drifted back over to peek curiously down through another open pit. "I believe it will be safer to bring them down with us than to have them fall upon our heads," the Vulcan said, with what appeared to be complete seriousness. The two youngest members of the party slid back from their positions with conscience-stricken looks. "And if Doctor McCoy's surmise about that flowstone mound is correct, we will need all available hands to excavate it."

Sulu glanced down ruefully at the empty right sleeve of his cave suit. "Maybe you should have brought that young captain of yours down here, after all."

"That would have been illogical." Spock swung himself onto the knotted rope and began to descend, his deep voice echoing up through the cavern's walls. "In the event that we find enough information to begin testing the alien time transporter, young James Kirk will be the last person we send through it. However, you, Captain Sulu, may very well be the first."

The Gorn shuttle took off vertically, with a jump so overpowered that it made Sulu's teeth snap together. He barely felt the pain of his bitten lip. The shock of hearing that he was already dead on this planet, in this time, had hit him with unexpected force. It wasn't dismay or disbelief that made Sulu's breath catch in his suddenly dry throat. It was the horror of realizing that the immense explosion he had been flung into was his own funeral pyre, that he had actually witnessed the moment of his other self's death. The first grinding moments of upward acceleration passed in a shuddering blur. It wasn't until the warm metallic tang of blood filled his mouth and forced him to swallow that Sulu was reminded that *he* was still alive. And that his presence here might be something more than just an insane and inexplicable nightmare.

"I died in that explosion," he said, more to himself than to Chekov. "And at that exact instant, I was sent here from another world and time. That has to mean something."

"Not to me," Chekov's blunt voice said from the helmet speaker pressed against his ear. The white hum of sound dampeners had canceled out all other sound, but Sulu could tell from the fuzzy look of the shuttle's inner walls that it was filled with engine noise. The Russian had sunk his hands deep into the sockets that seemed to control the vessel's pitch and speed, bracing his elbows against the bottom rim of the cockpit window to steady himself as his makeshift block stilts vibrated across the bare metal floor.

Sulu wiped a trickle of blood from his chin. "Chekov, listen—the alien transporter that threw me here must have somehow known that the Sulu in this time was about to die. What if it was trying to replace him, by sending me forward in time to that exact point?"

"What if it was?" the older man answered with surprising coldness. "What good did it do for you to come here, when you don't know a damned thing about the situation? If your alien machine had really wanted to help, it would have transported my captain out of the explosion so we could plan a new way to infiltrate and destroy Tesseract Fortress."

"I can help you do that," Sulu said, stung.

There was a pause as the Gorn shuttle switched over from vertical to horizontal motion with a lurch of uncompensated G-forces. "Maybe," Chekov said after he had wrestled the awkward ship into something resembling a level flight path. "But wasting time figuring out what your alien transporter did to you twenty years ago isn't going to destroy that Gorn installation any sooner."

Sulu gritted his teeth hard, both to protect them against the fierce reverberations now shaking the shuttle's bare metal frame and to keep from snapping back at the older man. He reminded himself that this Chekov had lived through a future so ghastly that Sulu could barely imagine it. It was understandable if his priorities didn't include puzzling out the mystery of Sulu's appearance here, much less trying to get him back to his proper place and time.

With a sigh that trickled out between his teeth, the young pilot realized he would have to depend on Uhura and the crew of the *Enterprise* back on Tlaoli to figure out how to return him to his own timeline. If his crewmates had noticed his disappearance, the way they had noticed Captain Kirk's, they might already be trying to discover where he had gone. There was always a chance they would figure out how to haul him back to his own time. Until then, there was nothing Sulu could do, stranded on this hostile alien planet with one hostile fellow human, except help prevent this horrifying future from getting any worse than it already was.

"You're heading back to the Gorn Fortress now?" he asked Chekov as he felt the Gorn shuttle lurch through the minor turbulence that marked an unseen range of hills below them.

"How did you—?" The Russian's suspicious voice broke off, then resumed again with a note of something that might have been amusement if it hadn't sounded so grim at the same time. "The captain always said he lost a lot of his pilot's instincts along with his reflexes after that first time the Gorn tortured him. This must be what he meant."

Sulu repressed a shudder at this glimpse into his own unpleasant future. "What are you planning to do? Bomb the Fortress from the air?"

"We tried that before we decided to infiltrate," Chekov answered impatiently. "We threw almost every weapon the *Hotspur* had at Tesseract after our ground forces were slaughtered. It never even shook them. You—the captain—thought the Gorn's transspace portal hub must be acting as its own shielding device, generating such a huge energy field that it warded off our attacks."

"So what's left?"

"Not much." There wasn't much left in the older man's voice, either. Even its grim tone had been leached away by sheer determination. "Just us and this shuttle."

Sulu glanced over his shoulder, bracing his feet into the vibrating metal struts of the parabolic wing, and saw the glowing darkness he'd been trying not to think about. God only knew how much subspace radiation was pouring out of that unshielded warp core, but one thing was certain. Without the layers of safety shielding, it wouldn't be hard to sabotage.

"But what about the timing? If it went off before the shuttle crashed—" Sulu wasn't even aware he was muttering out loud, until Chekov's voice answered in his ear.

"—the portal's shields would absorb most of the energy. We have to ride it down and crash just before the implosion."

Sulu craned a look up toward the man at the Gorn shuttle's primitive controls, startled again by the way he seemed able to pick unspoken thoughts out of Sulu's mind. "How did you know I was thinking about imploding the warp core?"

"Because it was what I was thinking about," Chekov said simply. "The captain and I tended to think about things the same way. Probably because I served under him for so many years."

It felt strange to have this older Chekov know him so well, when in his world he and the young Russian had barely met. But if he thought about it, he had to admit that he knew his own starship captain well enough to guess where his thoughts were going, except for those occasions where Kirk made one of his brilliant leaps of intuition that no one else could have either predicted or followed. And, oddly enough, Sulu felt as if he was beginning to know how to read this older version of Chekov in the same way. He hadn't even needed to ask, for instance, whether Chekov had realized that his plan of riding the shuttle down into the Gorn fortress meant they would both be killed in the warp core explosion. Somehow, he knew the older man understood and fully accepted the suicidal nature of his plan. That meant the only objections Sulu could raise to dissuade him would have to be pragmatic ones.

"If we implode the warp core at the same instant that we hit the fortress, you think the portal's shield will fail?"

"No, I think it will probably hold." There was emotion in Chekov's voice now, a note of distinctly Slavic irony and fatalism. "But it doesn't matter. This is the only thing left that I can think to do."

"It might not be the only thing *I* can think to do," Sulu pointed out.

There was a short pause in which Chekov might have snorted, although if he did the helmet's voice transmitter had edited out the wordless sound. Still, there was no doubt about the skepticism in his voice. "What could *you* possibly think of now that you couldn't also have thought of when we first landed here? That version of you had twenty years more experience with the Gorn."

Sulu winced, although he tried not to let his uncertainty show in his voice. "How can I know until I really see the Fortress? Maybe I won't think of anything, but all that means is that we'll have waited until sunrise and reconnoitered a little before we decide to crash and burn. Or is there some particular reason that you want to die right now?"

Sulu had meant the question to be sardonic, and he was a little surprised by the pause that followed, as if Chekov were actually mulling it over. His surprise deepened at the note of bitter amusement coloring the

Russian's voice when he finally spoke. "I always want to die right now. But there's no particular reason to hurry." He lifted one shoulder in an abbreviated shrug. "I suppose since I've waited this long to do it, another few hours won't kill me."

His last words sounded polished by use, like an old joke that had been repeated so often over the years it had become more of a motto than a punch line. Sulu wondered who had first dissuaded Chekov from committing suicide by tweaking his sense of humor and irony with that phrase. His own older self? It sounded like something he would say, but after seeing what this dismal future of torture and warfare had done to the enthusiastic young ensign he'd met on Tlaoli, Sulu wasn't even sure if he would recognize the captain he had supposedly become in this time and place.

Chekov swung the Gorn shuttle around in a jerky curve that made Sulu's teeth clack together again, this time snapping down on the soft inner skin of one cheek. He reclenched his jaws, this time being careful to speak between them. "Don't the Gorn believe in inertial dampeners?"

"They're from a much higher-gravity planet than Earth."

The shuttle lurched again, then settled into what seemed to be a circular holding pattern. The curving turns were still too fast and uncompensated to be restful, and Sulu carefully levered himself to his feet. "How many hours do we have to wait for sunrise?"

"About three."

Sulu nodded to himself. "That should be enough time," he muttered, this time intending Chekov to overhear. He wondered if the older man would be able to guess at his meaning again, but the Russian glanced down from his stilt-elevated height with a puzzled frown.

"Enough time for what?"

"For you to teach me how to fly this shuttle."

"Last panel, Carolyn," Uhura said. "Are you ready?"

"Ready." The blond archaeologist tapped a command into her translator that made its lights blink amber and red, then let it go so Uhura could begin hauling it up with the rope and pulley system they had fashioned for it. Not all of the purple-black metallic walls of the alien transporter chamber had writing on them, but the ones that did were inscribed from floor to ceiling with rows of ricelike script. In many places, curtains of translucent calcite had built up over the texts, and Sanner had to clamber up and down them wielding his rock hammer to remove the travertine. There was nothing they could do about the dark streaks of oxidation and tension fractures that had cut through other parts of the inscriptions. Uhura just hoped those missing sections didn't contain the most crucial information about Tlaoli's time transporter.

It had taken them over an hour to scan the nine panels of intricate runic script, and during that time Uhura had kept an apprehensive eye on the archaeological translator's power levels. They had brought chemical batteries with them as a backup, but she wasn't sure how many of the scans they would have to redo if they lost the instrument's original dilithium power cell. But so far, the portable magnetic shielding Spock had designed and Chief Engineer Scott had installed on all their instruments seemed to be holding power fluctuations and subspace interference at bay. The dedicated translator's processing unit had been humming away since the first panel was scanned, performing the trillions of cross-correlations it took to decipher a completely unknown alien language.

To Uhura's surprise, it had taken Spock and his work crew far less time to crack off the thick rind of flowstone that had built up around the alien transporter unit through uncounted millennia of being dripped on by runoff from the natural caves overhead. When it was freed from its crystalline chrysalis, the alien device was surprisingly simple to look at: a dozen interlaced and gyroscopically curved ellipses around a hollow inner space. With the travertine coating chipped away, the blue glow Sanner had been able to see only in total darkness settled down into a fierce sapphire flame visible even when all their carbide lights were turned toward it. Despite its increased brightness, the alien light seemed content to remain inside its dark metal cage for now, even when the Vulcan science officer deliberately set a spare dilithium cell next to it and watched its power leach away. The force field's glow intensified a little, but didn't seem to reach any farther toward the metal edges of its generator.

"Do you think it was never supposed to go any farther than this?" McCoy asked, watching the force field from outside the circle Spock had gouged in the lime mud of the cavern floor to mark the safety perimeter. "Maybe all that rock around it distorted the force field into reaching out farther than it was supposed to."

"I do not yet know enough about the device to draw any definite conclusions, Doctor," the Vulcan replied. "The force field has not seemed to change shape since we first removed the travertine from around it, but it is possible that the power required to charge it is so great that a single drained dilithium cell makes no detectable difference. I am loathe to let it drain any more cells before we have obtained more information on exactly what it might be doing."

Uhura lowered the translating device down across the last rows of inscribed letters, then swung it back toward Palamas. "Did it get everything scanned into its graphic memory?"

The archaeologist watched the data scroll across the translator's small screen. "All except for that crack across the top. I'll start the final semantic correlation as soon as these phonemes are done processing." She glanced across at Uhura. "We'll have to make an initial guess at gross linguistic structure to get the analysis started. You're the language expert.... What do you think?"

Uhura peered up at the rows of variably slanted rice grains that rose into darkness above them. At first glance, their similarity to primitive hieroglyphics invited her to see pictures in their geometric patterns, but the even spacing between groups warned her that it couldn't be that simple.

"Not pictorial," she said. "I'd guess phonetic, but perhaps based more on varying throat vibrations than lip and mouth sounds."

"All right." Palamas programmed their choice into the translator, then placed it down on the ground between them. "Now, all we can do is wait."

Uhura glanced over her shoulder, hearing a familiar emphatic voice rising from the other side of the cave.

"—first saw the field, it was all the way out to *here*." Sanner stamped on the small rise in the floor where Kirk and Chekov had been standing when they vanished. "And even after that first transport, it kept expanding, Commander. It sure looked to me like the power level was increasing."

"That would have been over an hour after it drained power from the *Enterprise*," Spock observed, "which implies a significant internal delay in the power storage rate."

"But the cave seemed to get colder almost instantaneously when we were firing our phasers in it," Uhura pointed out. "If Mr. Sanner is right about the power storage reaction being endothermic, shouldn't we have seen a delay in the temperature change, as well?"

The Vulcan lifted both eyebrows, a rare sign of appreciation for a particularly cogent point. "Indeed, Lieutenant. Let us assume that both those data points are valid. What does that tell us about the power consumption of this device?"

"That it processes in-phase energy more easily than out-of-phase energy," blurted a Russian voice from the far side of the device. As soon as he said it, Chekov looked as if he had startled even himself with that deduction, and he took a backward step that made him bump into Yuki Smith.

Spock's eyebrows might have gone up just a fraction further, but he acknowledged the young ensign's contribution without any other hint of surprise. "Precisely, Mr. Chekov. The fact that the alien device was able to absorb our transporter beam shows that it is designed to accept large inputs of energy from space. But the rapid processing of your much smaller phaser bursts suggests that its energy receptors are optimized for phase-aligned rather than frequency-distributed energy."

McCoy's carbide light emphasized the downward curve of his scowl, making him look more aggravated than he probably was. "Speak English, Spock. What does that mean for us?"

The Vulcan drummed his fingers on his tricorder, as if he disliked being pushed into making a conclusion on such limited data. After a moment, however, he sighed. "That we can probably control the device's power needs by hitting it with precisely timed phaser bursts from the *Enterprise*."

There was a moment of echoing silence, broken by

Sulu's calm voice. "Then are we ready to send the first test subject through this gate?"

"Hardly, Captain," said the Vulcan. "We still have no idea for what ultimate purpose this machine was designed, much less how to control and program it. If you stepped into this force field now, it might send you to a time period in your own past, rather than the future from which you came. We would then add another layer of time paradoxes to the ones which we are currently struggling to undo." He swung around, away from the fiery blue heart of the alien device and toward Uhura and Palamas. "Have we made any progress in translating the texts on these walls, Lieutenants?"

"Yes, sir." Palamas lifted the heavy translator and swung it forward so all of them could see the green status lights blinking to mark the completion of its program. "The bad news is that we only got a sixty-five percent correlation on this first run. We might be able to improve that by refining our linguistic analysis, but it could also be because of the missing parts of the text."

"Understood," said Spock.

Palamas handed the translator over to Uhura. "We requested a summary for each panel," Uhura said, and scrolled down through the output. "Panel one summarizes the geologic and biologic history of this planet, with a lot of emphasis on the fact that its natural resources had to be utterly depleted to cope with continued attacks from a powerful enemy empire. It seems to be almost an ethical defense of this civilization's treatment of their homeworld, in case the universe ever called them to account for it. The second and third panels summarize all the major battles and campaigns of this interstellar war, which lasted for approximately—" She paused for a moment, frowning at the translator screen in disbelief. "This can't be right. It says the war lasted for seven thousand years!"

"Maybe that was one of the places where you lost some text," McCoy suggested.

"Maybe." Uhura scrolled down to the next translator entry. "The fourth and fifth panel might be ones we need to read in detail. The translator found them hard to summarize, because they contain a lot of numbers and equations and references to quantum subspace magnetism." She glanced curiously up at Spock. "I didn't think magnetic fields existed in subspace."

"According to our latest subspace field theories, they do not," the Vulcan said. "But most subspace physicists would agree that our current theories are neither complete nor entirely correct. What do the other panels deal with?"

Uhura read through the next description once, blinked, then read through it a second time to make sure she hadn't misunderstood. "Panels six and seven seem to be another list of battles, very similar to the ones listed on panels two and three. But the translator seems to think that these battles were somehow fought a second time, in an attempt to alter their original outcome."

McCoy whistled softly. "They discovered time travel," he said. "I bet *that's* what all those subspace magnetic field equations were about. And once they could travel in time, they went back and tried to intervene in their own history."

"They must have been losing the war," Palamas said.

"Or winning in such a way that it wasn't worth the cost," Sulu added in a grim voice.

"Did it work?" asked Yuki Smith. "Did they save their civilization?"

Uhura scrolled down to the next panel, then shook her head. "It doesn't look like it. Panel eight says that their enemies also began crossing through time, striking blows in places where they weren't expected. Then it describes a desperate phase in the war, when the aliens were so low on combatants and stretched across so many fronts in time that they began to recycle their soldiers through time. As each soldier healed up from battle injuries, they were sent back through time to the point where they'd been injured, so they could continue fighting that battle a little longer. The injured version they replaced was brought back here to be healed and sent out again." She glanced up from the translator, frowning. "By the end, it says they had only a few hundreds of soldiers, each one fighting almost alone on a different battlefield in time."

"So they lost the war?" Smith asked mournfully.

"Yes." Uhura scrolled down to the ninth and last panel summary. "There were still civilians left on this planet, though. The last panel says they used their regular time-traveling devices to escape into the far distant future, setting the machinery to self-destruct behind them so their enemies couldn't track them down. But they left behind this Janus Gate on purpose. The last part of the panel explains that the natives wanted to give this technology to whatever spacefaring race came to the planet after them, in recompense for exhausting all of this world's natural resources."

There was a long silence after she was done. Sulu was the first to break it. "The Janus Gate?" he asked, curiously.

Uhura looked to Carolyn Palamas for help, and the archaeologist sighed. "This translator is programmed to provide mythopoetic equivalents wherever appropriate," she explained. "It's meant to give us a sense of the larger cultural connotations raised when a modern civilization deliberately uses an archaic myth or god as a name for something. In this case, the name of the Roman god of gates and doorways is clearly meant to invoke—"

"The ability to travel forward and backward in time," Spock finished for her. "A bit ethnocentric, Lieutenant, is it not? You could have chosen the name of the ancient Vulcan goddess who presided over the opening and closing of festivals—"

"I don't care if we name it after Woody Woodpecker!" McCoy burst out. "I want to know what we're going to do with it now that we know what it was for."

"Use it, of course." The Vulcan turned his head to regard the older version of Sulu with an unblinking regard. "I presume you are willing to be returned to your battle, now that you have been healed, Captain Sulu?"

"More than willing," Sulu said. "Just as long as you give me something I can use to blow myself up as soon as I get there."

Chapter Seven

SUNRISE ARRIVED with unexpected violence on Basaraba. The mists that filled the hollows between the planet's cloud-forested ridges curdled up into massive thunderheads just before dawn, and the occasional rain showers Sulu had torn through as he painfully learned how to pilot the Gorn shuttle merged and thickened into a downpour. Lightning flashed across the graying sky, each time leaving it a little brighter than before, as if the sky had to be hacked apart to admit the rising sun. Sulu's sound-dampening helmet drowned out the rolls of thunder that presumably followed, just as it muffled the drumming of rain on the shuttle's uninsulated hull. But he knew the storm was peaking when the Gorn shuttle's parabolic wings began to catch and twist in the churning turbulence. Sulu let the ship flit upward with each gust of wind, then allowed gravity to drift it back into place without ever needing to apply a blast from its overpowered warp engines.

"You already fly this thing better than I do." Chekov's transmitted voice put no more emotion into that praise than he had put into any of the criticisms he'd made when Sulu was first getting the hang of the hand-manipulated flight controls. The Russian hadn't objected to teaching him how to fly the Gorn shuttle, although Sulu wasn't sure if he'd done it for tactical reasons or just because he was bored at the prospect of spending three hours hovering in darkness before immolating himself. "I think I'll let you take it into the Fortress."

"You think crashing it will take a lot of piloting ability?"

His helmet communicator didn't transmit Chekov's snort, but Sulu could feel the gust of air against the back of his neck. The older man had strapped on a second pair of block stilts so he could share the clear cockpit dome that had been designed to fit around one larger Gorn skull. He craned his head past Sulu now, peering through the staccato flash of lightning toward the Gorn fortress. They could just see its towers and outspread ramparts emerging in the distance, a darker blotch against the predawn charcoal wash of forest and sky.

"No, I meant right now, when we go in to reconnoiter. You remember what not to do?"

The question was so curt it sounded hostile, but

Sulu had grown used to the older man's teaching style by now. "Don't leave a wake trail that one of their shuttles could use to track us," he answered promptly. "I'll go in low enough for our wake to feel like thermal updrafts from the ground."

"What else?"

"No sudden blasts of acceleration that might set off their ion detectors. No passes close to open windows where they might feel our draft."

"What else?"

Sulu racked his brain to think of other ways the Gorn shuttle could be detected despite the Romulan-designed cloaking device that Chekov assured him couldn't be picked up by sensor or by sight. If all it cloaked was the sound of its own warp engines—

"No breaking the sound barrier?" Sulu guessed.

"Right. And what speed is that on this planet?"

Sulu opened his mouth, then closed it again. There were too many variables of air temperature, density, and composition for him to estimate it. "I don't know."

"I don't, either," Chekov admitted. "But it seems to be a little higher than Mach 1. Stay under the limit you know and you'll be fine."

"Yes, sir," Sulu said and felt another puff of air hit his neck from Chekov's unheard snort. The first time he'd addressed the older man as the superior officer he actually was, Sulu had felt Chekov silently shaking at his back. It had taken him a while to realize that with his face so badly scarred, the Russian couldn't let his laughter out any other way. Even now, after hours of hearing it, the honorific still seemed to amuse his companion. "Should we go now?"

Chekov glanced back at the eastern horizon. The worst of the storm had passed, opening up a slash of silver-blue sky behind it, but rain still splattered down from above them. "Let's wait until the sky clears all the way overhead. I'm not sure how well the visual deception screens can mimic rain when we're flying through it."

Sulu nodded and kept the shuttle in its low-altitude hover until the last of the clouds had scudded past. A golden gleam of sunlight spilled over the encircling ridges and touched the top of the tallest Gorn tower. Its silhouette looked clean and stark against the storm clouds, showing no trace of damage from the explosion that had rocked it the previous day.

"Why do you call it Tesseract Fortress?" Sulu asked Chekov, mostly to break the silence that felt like it was slowly coiling into a tense knot. The Russian didn't seem to notice it as much. When he answered, his voice in Sulu's helmet sounded almost relaxed.

"It was the closest English word Uhura could find to match what the Gorn called it. You know what a tesseract is?"

"A four-dimensional cube."

"Uhura said the Gorn name for this place was ambiguous—one part of it meant 'multiple dimensions,' another part meant either 'enclosure' or 'entrapment.' We needed to call it something, and Tesseract seemed as good a name as any."

Sulu glanced down at the shuttle's minimal control board. All the primitive knobs and levers there controlled the warp engines and the Romulan cloaking device. There was a speaker panel that occasionally startled him with a burst of growled-out Gorn commands but no way to alter the frequency it was set at or to speak back through it. The Gorn apparently saw no need for their fighter pilots to report in, or to know anything more than they chose to tell them. "You listened in on the Gorn's communications?"

"From the *Hotspur.*" Chekov's voice rasped with a faint tinge of what might have been disgust. "Uhura did most of that. Neither Sulu nor I can listen to Gorn for long without throwing up. It's an aftereffect of the drugs they used when they tortured us back in '78." He paused. "I probably shouldn't have told you that."

"Why not?" Sulu asked dryly. "It doesn't look as if I'm going to live long enough to have it happen to me."

"But that can't be right," Chekov said slowly, as if the time paradox had just occurred to him. "If you don't live through this and get back to your own time, how can I remember you being my captain?"

Sulu gritted his teeth against an urge to remind the other man that *he'd* been the one who'd cut off any attempt to discuss this question a few hours ago. "I don't know," Sulu said. "Maybe we're not from the same dimension of reality. You and I remember two completely different captains on the *Enterprise.*"

"True." Chekov paused again. "Do you still want

to help me destroy Tesseract Fortress, even if this isn't your own reality?"

"Yes," Sulu said before he could even think about it. A moment later, he realized where that instinctive agreement came from. "I swore an oath when I was commissioned as a Starfleet officer, to protect and defend the Federation. That oath is just as binding here as anywhere else."

"In this reality," Chekov said grimly, "*nothing* would protect the Federation more than destroying Tesseract Fortress."

"Phasers locked on target," said a crackling Scottish voice through Uhura's communicator unit. Magnetic shielding might keep their equipment powered up and operating smoothly, but there was nothing it could do about the interference Tlaoli's strange energy fields injected into the subspace continuum between them and the ship. "Awaiting your order, Commander."

"Fire when ready," said Spock calmly.

Uhura stood on tiptoe in an attempt to see past the Vulcan, but Sulu and McCoy stood shoulder to shoulder behind him, blocking the entrance to the Janus Gate. Just as they had after losing Captain Kirk, the entire caving team had retreated for safety into the alien conduit system that connected this chamber to the other parts of the Tlaoli caves. One previous phaser strike had already turned the air inside the transport chamber colder, making the mist condense back into an icy rind across the walls. The alien light that burned inside the transporter device had deepened to the intense cobalt blue of a photon emission laser, but there was still no sign of the drifting light curtains that had filled the room the first time they had been here.

"Firing," said Chief Engineer Scott. A second later, Uhura felt the ground around her shake with the impact of the ship's powerful weapons. A wave of bitter cold seemed to wash past them without any gust of wind, leaving Uhura almost breathless with the effort it took to breathe the suddenly frigid air. A few moments later, rock fell with a clatter somewhere in the travertine-lined conduit behind her.

"I think we're losing some ceiling integrity back here," called Sanner's muffled voice from farther down the conduit. "You guys better keep your helmets on."

McCoy snorted. "Spock, do you think we could set the phasers to stun those rocks rather than kill them?"

The Vulcan glanced over his shoulder, and Uhura was startled to see that his sharply angled eyebrows had turned white with frost. "So far, we have not even succeeded in expanding the alien force field past its metal containment walls," he said. "The amount of energy required to recharge the transporter may well exceed the structural strength of the overlying rock deposits."

"But, Mr. Spock, it already seems much colder in here than it did when we lost Captain Kirk." The temperature-sensitive nano-fibers in Uhura's caving suit had expanded to their maximum thickness, but she could still feel the cold biting at her skin. "The light from the force field is brighter, too."

Chekov cleared his throat in the shadows behind her. "That could be because we took off its flowstone cover, Lieutenant."

"Or because I'm right and the force field is *supposed* to stay inside the transporter device." McCoy poked Spock in the shoulder, and Uhura saw the tall Vulcan wince. "Come on, Spock, admit I could be right for once."

The Vulcan looked back at the brilliant sapphire fire whose glittering reflections danced off all the chamber's ice-sheathed walls. "Your hypothesis is gaining credibility, Doctor," he admitted. "But according to my calculations, we have so far charged the device with only thirty percent of the energy it was able to drain from the *Enterprise*. Unless we can establish that it was overcharged before, or that its travertine shell deformed its force field in the past, we cannot know what the current status of the Janus Gate device truly represents."

There was a silence, full only of the raspy breathing of eight people trying not to draw in too much of the ice-cold air. Then, from one side, Uhura heard a tentatively cleared throat.

"Commander Spock," said Yuki Smith. "Do you think maybe those blinking lights over there could help us figure that out?"

The Vulcan scanned the entire chamber, his lean face silhouetted by its steady cobalt glow. "I do not observe any blinking lights, Mr. Smith. Where do you perceive them to be?"

"Reflected off that back wall over there." The security guard shouldered past Chekov and Sanner to point the way. Uhura tried to peer in the direction she indicated, but the fiery sapphire glare of the Janus Gate was all she could see reflected in the ice-sheathed wall. Yuki Smith's initial confidence seemed to deflate a little beneath their baffled looks. "Maybe I'm just not seeing things right because I'm color-blind. But it still looks to me like something's blinking—"

Spock gave the security guard a thoughtful look, then lifted his tricorder and angled it in the direction she had pointed. After a moment, he glanced at the screen and gave a single, decisive nod. "Something is indeed blinking back there, Mr. Smith. But it is blinking in a yellow-green wavelength that to our eyes is completely obscured by the cyan emissions of the force field. Thank you for bringing it to my attention."

"You're welcome, sir." Smith fell back beside Chekov, giving him a surreptitious punch as if to say "I win." Uhura had just enough time to see the young Russian grimace in response before her attention was torn away by a sharp protest from McCoy.

"Spock, you're not going in there!"

The Vulcan science officer paused a meter into the ice-walled chamber. "Someone needs to investigate that blinking light, Doctor," he said. "I believe I can read my own tricorder well enough to avoid stepping into a subspace rift."

Uhura took a quick and painfully cold breath, then reached out to take the archaeological translator from Carolyn Palamas. "And I think I can stay close enough behind you to be safe, too." Both McCoy and Sulu swung around to give her disapproving looks, and Uhura held the translator up in front of herself like a shield. "If that light pattern turns out to be some type of communication in the ancient Tlaoli language, we need to know what it's saying."

"I concur," Spock said, before the others could respond. "You may accompany me, Lieutenant, but be prepared to retreat quickly in the event I issue an alert."

"Aye, sir." Uhura was already prepared to retreat—it was being prepared to advance any closer to that eerie alien light that she wasn't so sure about. But by keeping her gaze fixed firmly on the icy cave floor, as if she wanted to make sure of her footing, she managed to follow Spock out into the chamber without any apparent hesitation.

The Vulcan charted a deliberate spiral path around the Janus Gate, watching his tricorder's screen closely as they approached it from behind. Uhura could hear the instrument chattering softly in the silence, and realized Spock must have activated an audible as well as visible record of the subspace instability in the room. That made it a little easier for her to follow him. As they approached the curving metal bulk of the alien transporter, the air grew so bitterly cold that Uhura could feel the inside of her throat begin to ache. She lifted her free hand up to her face and began to breath through the material of her glove.

If Spock noticed the painful chill, he gave no sign. "Subspace readings remain marginal," he said as they began to circle behind the Janus Gate. He spoke loudly enough that Uhura knew the communication was meant as much for their teammates back in the conduit as it was for her. "I am beginning to see the blinking lights that Mr. Smith detected. The source appears to be a panel attached to this side of the alien device."

"A *control* panel?" McCoy demanded, his voice echoing off the icy walls.

"Possibly, Doctor." Spock came to a halt a meter away from the dark metallic structure whose curving elliptical arms enclosed a heart of incandescent fire. He consulted with his tricorder, then glanced over his shoulder at Uhura. "There is an increased probability of subspace rifts on either side of us, Lieutenant," he said in a quiet voice designed not to carry across the chamber. "But there appears to be a safe pathway leading toward that panel. You will need to walk precisely where I do to remain inside it."

"Aye, sir." Uhura swung her bulky translator around and hugged it in front of her, to make sure it wouldn't accidentally touch a subspace rift and be torn away. Spock nodded approval, and did the same thing with his own instrument, tilting it up against his chest so he could continue to watch its subspace readings as he turned and began to approach the

Janus Gate. Uhura followed him, careful to place her feet in the dark bar of his shadow. She could no longer catch a glimpse of the tricorder's flashing screen, but she could hear how its gentle chattering had slowed to an almost inaudible hum. "Are the readings getting lower, Mr. Spock?"

"Indeed, they are. I suspect we are approaching a protected station where an operator is meant to stand." Spock came to a halt in front of the panel, whose blinking green-gold lights could be seen easily from this side, and swung his tricorder around in a careful arm's-length arc. Its low hum never varied. "I believe it is safe for you to stand here with me, Lieutenant."

"Spock, are you still out there?" McCoy's voice sounded more exasperated than anxious. "If you are, could you please let us know what the blazes is going on?"

"We have reached the control panel, Doctor, and are proceeding to analyze it." Spock scanned his tricorder across the polished indigo metal with its multiple rows of rice-shaped lights. It looked very different from the dark and roughened surface of the main transporter device behind it. "I do not recall seeing anything like this when we first chipped away the flowstone mound," Spock observed. "This part of the device must have been stored for protection, and released when we began to charge the machine's energy banks."

Uhura's eyes hadn't left the intricately flashing rows of lights with their familiar ricelike shapes. "Mr.

Spock, I think those lights are flashing the same kinds of phonemes we saw on the chamber's walls. If I could lift my translator up to scan them—"

Instead of moving out of her way, the Vulcan science officer lifted the bulky translator for her and held it effortlessly at shoulder height while Uhura adjusted the visual scanning rate to adjust for the strobe rate of the blinking lights. English words immediately began scrolling down the translator's main display screen, and Spock angled his head so he could read them along with Uhura.

Status Report: field strength at maximal levels, reserve power buffered at maximal capacity, field integrity optimized for (word unknown) transport. Full transfer mode engaged, viewing mode disengaged, associative transport disengaged, activity buffer (word unknown, word unknown) error in reading file.

"Fascinating," said Spock. "This certainly answers our question about whether the machine requires any more power to be input into it."

"But what do you suppose it means by viewing mode and associative transport?" Uhura asked.

"I do not yet know." Spock put out a tentative hand and touched one of the slightly raised bars on the right side of the panel. As he pressed it, the flashing lights first went dark, then began to pulse again, although this time only one of the rows was lit. Uhura glanced at the translator's display screen. *"Associative transport engaged,"* she read to Spock, whose attention was now on the alien transporter device itself. The fiery glow at its center blossomed suddenly into a paler veil of light that washed out across the entire chamber. Uhura's breath froze in her throat, and she heard a chorus of alarmed shouts from the other side of the chamber. But the blue glow splashed around the control panel as if an invisible seawall held it back, and nothing happened to her and Spock.

"We're all right!" she shouted to the rest of the team, seeing that Spock was too engrossed in his observations to bother reassuring them. "We're testing the machine's controls. Stay where you are."

"How about if we move a little farther away?" McCoy snapped. "That blue light just about nipped off my nose!"

"Undoubtedly because the appendage in question was being put where it should not have been," Spock said almost absently. Fortunately, his voice wasn't loud enough for the doctor to hear. "I believe I now understand the meaning of 'associative transport,' Lieutenant Uhura. In that mode, the subspace rift expands outward so more than just a single person can be sent to the same point in time. That would have been an advantage if the ancient Tlaoli needed to send an entire platoon of soldiers back to a battle from which a single survivor had been plucked."

"I think you're right." Uhura had finally pulled her gaze away from the billowing sea of light, and noticed that the indicator lights had added a second row of words. "The translator says, '*Power insufficient for more than fifteen (word unknown) to be conveyed.*' It can't determine if that Tlaoli measuring unit refers to weight, mass, or just amount."

"Since we do not need to transfer more than a single person back to his rightful place in time, that should not impede us." Spock pressed the second of the raised control bars, and the blue light slowly contracted again, folding itself back into the hollow center of the Janus Gate. Its sapphire glow was no longer steady, however. It had begun to flicker, not as randomly as a candle flame but in a slow visual sine wave that shifted from brighter to darker shades as it repeated itself.

" '*Viewing mode engaged,*' " Uhura read from the alien display. This time she waited to see if the control panel would add a second line to the first. After a moment, it did. "*Time and distance variation enabled.*"

"Additional controls are emerging," Spock said, and Uhura glanced over to see two new vertical bars flex up beneath the panel's blue-violet metallic skin. "Viewing mode with time and distance variation... Perhaps this function allowed the ancient Tlaoli to select a particular time and place for transport when there were multiple crisis points from which to choose."

"That would make sense," said Sulu's voice. "Why send someone back to a hopeless situation if there was a previous point that might change that entire branch of the timeline?"

"Indeed, I agree—" Spock's voice broke off at the same moment that Uhura swung around, suddenly aware that the resonant voice of their former pilot had been much too clear to be coming from the conduit. She saw Sulu standing just outside the safety perimeter Spock had drawn in the wet lime mud of the floor, now transformed into a gleaming ring of thicker and whiter ice. He had casually slung across his shoulder the spare backpack which Sanner had loaded with all of their emergency rock explosives, and was gazing into the flickering heart of the time transporter with his odd, bittersweet smile.

"You are disregarding orders, Mr. Sulu," said the Vulcan.

"You can't give orders to a superior officer, Mr. Spock," the older man reminded him gently. "And time is running out. Are you ready to try sending me back to Basaraba?"

Spock eyed the other man for a long moment. "Assuming that we have interpreted the Janus Gate correctly and can view the future before we transport you into it…yes, Captain. I believe I am ready to make that attempt."

"Good." Sulu glanced around the machine. "When the field expanded a few moments ago, I noticed that there seems to be another clear space on the opposite side of this ellipse. Shall I try standing in it?"

"Yes. Be certain to walk directly in toward it from the perimeter line. You may not be *required* to obey that order," he added dryly, "but if you do not, you may encounter an errant subspace rift that will not respect your rank."

"Spock, are you sure about this?" McCoy demanded from the edge of the conduit. "If we lose this Sulu and can't get our version back again—"

"—then we will have lost only a single crewman from the *Enterprise*," the Vulcan finished bluntly. "It is a risk we must take, Doctor. We need to know how to operate this machine, so that we can return young James Kirk safely to his proper time. We have very little of our own time left in which to do so."

"And the fate of the Federation may be determined by how well we do it." Sulu walked the gleaming line of the safety perimeter until he disappeared from Uhura's view, then reappeared on the far side of the Janus Gate. In its flickering blue glow, Sulu already looked more like a ghost than a person. "Spock, I can see what looks like a set of handgrips on this side of the Gate. Should I take hold of them?"

"I would advise you to," the Vulcan replied. "They are no doubt meant to keep you within a safely protected space."

Sulu stepped forward without hesitation, lifting his left hand to wrap around one of the gleaming metal bars in front of him, then, after a moment's thought, resting his severed right wrist on the other. "It feels like it's vibrating a little," he reported after a moment. "Nothing else seems to be happening."

"That is because I have not yet engaged the controls which vary time and distance." Spock bent over the control panel again. "Lieutenant Uhura, please alert me immediately to any change in the message displays, even before you get a translation for it," he ordered. "Captain Sulu, I would like you to report continuously on what you see and feel. If you suspect at any time that you are about to be pulled into a time and place that is not Basaraba, shout an alarm. The viewing mode we are about to employ seems to be a partially disabled version of the actual Janus Gate transfer mechanism. It should be safe, but I calculate a seventeen point three percent probability that you may be transferred without my changing the settings on the device."

"Understood." Sulu braced himself a little more securely in place, stiffening his shoulders to keep his pack of rock explosives balanced on his back. Despite his rigid posture, the flickering blue light showed his creased face looking neither anxious nor determined, but actually more relaxed than Uhura could remember having seen it before. She tried once again to imagine what kind of life this Hikaru Sulu must have lived to make his final plunge through time to self-destruction a moment of tranquility and comfort, but her mind simply couldn't encompass it. Instead, she tore her gaze away from him and concentrated on watching the translator's screen for the first hint of a new message.

"I am engaging the time controls," Spock said. The force field's glow increased both in brightness and in the frequency of its flicker, and little runnels of cobalt light began to streak across the inside of the elliptical metal cage that held it confined. Uhura squashed an instinctive desire to take a step back from that glowing metal structure. She could see the quicksilver light streaks spiraling to the outside of the Janus Gate now, cutting brighter paths through its crust of oxidized metal as they went. A moment later, the handgrips Sulu held were also netted in strands of light, and the glow did not stop there. It laced itself slowly up Sulu's arms, across his shoulders, and then up like a spiderweb across his face.

"Spock, why have you sent me here?" the older man demanded sharply. "This isn't Basaraba!"

"You have gone nowhere, Captain. Despite what you may see, you are still physically present on Tlaoli."

Sulu turned his blue-netted face around, eyes open but suddenly seeming blind. "I can hear you, but I can't see anything but this ship. What ship is this? It's not the *Hotspur*—oh, God, I know it! It's that Klingon warship, the *Kerzhat,* that we served aboard as a prize crew after the battle at Mirk's World. The Klingons chased after us to destroy it, and if the *Hotspur* hadn't caught up to us again we wouldn't have made it out alive—"

"Message appearing," Uhura said urgently. "The translator says, '*Major crisis point located within five [word unknown] units of time. Question send/not send.*'"

Spock nodded, watching the lacework of blue light pulse around their former helmsman. "If I pushed the third transfer bar now, I believe the light would engulf him and cause him to vanish. I moved the time control only a tiny fraction, assuming that it had many millennia of play built into it. Let me try moving it a little more." Long Vulcan fingers moved on the control panel with intent delicacy, and the blue net of light swirled briefly around Sulu's still figure, then settled into a different braided pattern. "Where are you now, Captain?"

"At the battle of Borsdal Kren," said the older man grimly. "We almost lost the *Hotspur* to a hull breach there."

"The translator says, '*Major crisis point located within twelve [word unknown] units of time. Question send/not send.*' "

"You're getting closer." Sulu seemed a little calmer now, as if he'd realized that he wasn't really where he seemed to be. "Basaraba should be six years further into the future."

"I will attempt to calibrate as best I can." It didn't even seem to Uhura as if Spock's fingers had moved on the controls, but she could see the cobalt glitter as the net of liquid light swirled around Sulu once again. "Are you there yet?"

"*Yes.*" Sulu's voice took on a suddenly hard-wrenched note. "I'm in Tesseract Keep, right where I was when they shot us down. I think I see Uhura—"

Uhura took a deep breath as she read the translator's screen. " '*Terminal crisis point located,*' " she said softly, although she wasn't sure why. It wasn't as if Sulu didn't know this was the end of his life. " *'Question send/not send.'* "

Spock's left hand moved slightly on the other control. "I am adjusting the distance controls, Captain Sulu. Where are you now?"

"Inside the corridor that leads to the portal hub!" the older man said. "I must be past the place where they caught us. I can hear shooting in the distance behind me."

"Is this a safe place to send you?" Spock inquired. Uhura gave him a baffled look—given the future Sulu was going back to, there was no such thing as a safe place to be sent—but she heard the older pilot take a deep breath of what sounded like relief as he replied.

"Yes, this is perfect. It looks like I'm beyond the main Gorn checkpoint. Even without weapons, I think I can make it all the way into the portal from here. Send me, Spock."

The Vulcan moved one hand from the vertical bars that controlled distance and time to the horizontal ones that determined whether the person on the other side merely saw a point in their future or were sent rocketing toward it. "Engaging transport mode now," was all he said.

Uhura held her breath as the blue light in the center of the Janus Gate blazed up from its subdued flicker to a phaser-bright glare. The runnels of light wrapped around Sulu suddenly expanded outward and coalesced, wrapping him in a sheath of cobalt flame... then abruptly flung themselves off again.

Sulu blinked once, like a man regaining his vision after seeing too bright a light, then focused on them across the steady glow of the alien force field. "I'm still here."

"Indeed," said Mr. Spock. "It appears as if the Janus Gate has decided not to send you back to your future after all."

Chapter Eight

"HOW CAN THE MACHINE 'decide' not to send him?" McCoy leaned precariously around the edge of the conduit's mouth, squinting against the icy blue glow still filling the chamber. "Isn't sending people through time what it was built to do?"

Chekov resisted an urge to grab the doctor by the belt and drag him back around the corner to safety. He'd already had his hands slapped once for trying to politely restrain McCoy while Spock first tested the device, and had a feeling he might actually get yelled at this time if he tried to intervene. Instead, he came carefully up alongside McCoy in the entrance, where he might be in position to "accidentally" get in the way if McCoy tried to go any farther into the cavern.

"Spock, maybe you read the instructions wrong."

Uhura looked up from where she and Spock had drawn together over her translator. Chekov wasn't sure if it was anger or frustration that sharpened her normally gentle voice. "If anyone read the instructions wrong, Doctor McCoy, it was me. I was doing the translating."

"But Spock's the one twiddling the knobs."

"I do not believe anyone has made an error." The doctor's criticism made no apparent impact on the first officer. Spock's eyes never shifted from their study of the glowing console, his face beneath the wash of blue light as impassive as ever. "I believe the device functioned precisely as it was designed."

McCoy took a short step forward, turning almost immediately into a tight circle as better sense overrode his instinct to pace into the Vulcan's line of sight. "How can that be? You said it was designed to send soldiers into combat."

"*Healthy* soldiers."

At first, Sulu didn't even look up to acknowledge the attention suddenly cast in the direction of his comment. He stood, barely visible on the opposite curve of the device, with his hand closed around his foreshortened right arm and the pack of rock explosives hanging heavily from his back. For the first time Chekov could remember, the competent, battle-hardened captain from their future looked inexpressibly weary and old.

"Healthy soldiers," Sulu said again, holding up his empty sleeve in silent explanation. "I apparently don't count as a healthy soldier anymore."

Chekov felt an unexpected despair kick him weakly in the stomach. Until that moment, he hadn't realized how much he'd been counting on this transfer to work. How much hope he'd invested in their being able to easily exchange both Sulu and Kirk for their proper counterparts and thus set the world to rights again. It was all he could do to keep from turning away and retreating into the conduit in disappointment.

"But you're the only soldier we've got!" McCoy's objection sounded angry instead of forlorn, but Chekov thought he heard the same desperation in the doctor's words. "Are you saying that there's no time in the future when our Sulu runs into one of your Gorn and needs pulling out? Wouldn't replacing him with a Sulu with no hand be better than not replacing him at all?"

"Apparently," Spock answered calmly, "the device does not think so."

Carolyn Palamas edged a little ways closer to the mouth of the conduit, lifting her soft voice almost apologetically so that it might carry into the cavern beyond. "The original builders must have had some cutoff at which they thought it was no longer to their advantage to keep..." She shrugged, as though unhappy that she couldn't think of a better term. "...recycling a combatant."

"But a *hand*...!"

Sulu interrupted McCoy's protest. "For me it's just a hand, Doctor. A hand I lost because the alien medical equipment couldn't sufficiently recognize it to figure out how to put it back together." The glance he aimed down at the missing limb was more regretful than bitter. "Who knows what the device thinks I've lost?"

Yuki Smith raised her hand tentatively, like a student in class a little afraid of offering something stupid to the discussion. "Does this mean we aren't going to be able to send the captain back?" She tucked her hand in quickly when everyone turned to look at her. "I mean, is the device ever going to think a fourteen-year-old kid is better than the full-grown Captain Kirk?"

Spock seemed to consider the question for a moment. "That is an issue we will confront after we have retrieved Lieutenant Sulu from the future," he said at last.

McCoy snorted. "Which you intend to do how, Spock?"

It was Lieutenant Uhura who volunteered the answer. "By sending someone else." She tipped her tricorder so that Spock could read the screen. "The associative transport function doesn't just take troops with you into battle," she explained aloud to the others while the Vulcan studied her translation, "it also allows you to bring troops *back* for reassignment elsewhere. Which means you should be able to retrieve both me and Lieutenant Sulu from the future, as long as I can find him."

Sulu shook his head. "You can't go."

"I'm the obvious choice," she countered. "You said I was with you…at the end. That means I should arrive close to the same time and place as our Lieutenant Sulu did, which should make it easy for me to locate him. I won't need to be there more than a few minutes."

"You won't *have* a few minutes," Sulu said. "Uhura, we were absolutely surrounded when you and I were killed. The only reason it would work to send me is because I didn't care if it killed me to go. Your Sulu would have been sent back to you, and I would have died, but it would have been *over.* I didn't have to try and reach someone and bring them back intact." He shook his head again, more sadly this time. "Even if he's standing right at your shoulder, Uhura, I don't think you'd be able to retrieve him fast enough."

Uhura met his gaze without flinching, although her voice betrayed her frustration. "But we have to try *something.*"

"I'll go." Chekov didn't realize he'd spoken aloud until everyone turned to stare at him. He fought down a blush, but continued, "You said I wasn't there in the fortress with you—I was in a shuttle up above."

Sulu surprised him with an ironic, lopsided smile. "You were in a shuttle that you were planning to crash into the Fortress as a diversion."

Chekov answered his smile with a shrug. "So Mr. Spock will make sure I transfer in just before that happens, and I won't crash. If Lieutenant Sulu survived being transported into the battle at all, I'll at least have some time to look for him." He looked back and forth from Sulu, to McCoy, to Uhura, surprised and a little angry at the skepticism he saw on all their faces. "I can do this. I want to."

"Do you know how to fly a Gorn shuttle?" Sulu made no effort to hide the sarcasm in his question.

"I can fly a Starfleet shuttle," Chekov countered. "I'm sure you can explain the differences well enough to keep me from crashing if I don't want to."

No one said anything for a long moment, then Sulu laughed softly and rubbed at his eyes as he shook his head. "And I thought the stubbornness came later."

"My mother would disagree."

At the mouth of the conduit, Smith raised her hand again and edged up next to Chekov. "Can't we at least send him with a phaser or something?"

"Good idea. Send us both with phasers." Sulu grinned at Chekov as he boldly stepped away from the console and into the ocean of blue light that could no longer threaten him while he was on his own. "I may not be able to replace myself," he told Chekov, "but I'll bet we can use that associative transport function to send me along as your backup. And you're going to need someone who knows the territory."

Much as he didn't want to admit it, Chekov also knew he'd be relieved to have the company. "All right."

Spock motioned him forward by sketching the path around the edge of the transport field with an economical sweep of his arm. "Then if Mr. Chekov would care to join us at the console"—he centered himself on the device and awoke the strange controls —"I believe the future is waiting."

* * *

"It looks like the sky's clear. Let's go."

Sulu balanced himself a little more carefully on his wooden stilts and dug his fingers deeper into the manipulative hollow designed for reptilian claws. The shuttle's warp engines responded with their usual rough surge of power, but he was ready for it now and angled the flaps on the parabolic wings to transform the jerk of upward motion into a smooth forward thrust. The Gorn shuttle sailed out over broad-leaved treetops that sparkled with sunlit pools of rain, heading for the perimeter walls of Tesseract Fortress. It was amazing, considering how short and frenzied his first flight over this alien landscape had been, how indelibly those crenulated walls had carved themselves into his memory. Sulu repressed an urge to slam the shuttle into faster flight, or to take evasive action. As hard as it was for him to believe, he had the evidence of his bruised and aching forehead to assure him that the Romulan cloaking device really did make the shuttle invisible to eyes and sensors. They would only be noticed if he did something stupid, like fly too fast or too close to an open window.

Even knowing that, however, it took all the self-control Sulu possessed to guide the Gorn shuttle into a slow, low-altitude circle above Tesseract Fortress with its outward pointing rows of projectile weapons. He could feel the sweat gathering again under his rain-damp uniform tunic, although this time it was from sheer anxiety and not exertion. *Pretend you're a hawk, soaring on a thermal current,* he told himself.

But the ferocious vibration of the overpowered aircraft he was piloting made that illusion hard to maintain.

"The portal hub is located underground, between those two tallest towers," said Chekov's emotionless voice inside his helmet. "When we crash the shuttle, we'll have to take it straight down between them to avoid getting caught up by the wings."

The bleak reminder that Sulu's lifespan in this future reality depended on coming up with an alternate plan for destroying the Gorn fortress suddenly made the shuttle's flight path seem a lot less important. Sulu began peering out through the curved cockpit window at the stone fortress below, letting his subconscious mind worry about balancing thrust and velocity and aerodynamic lift. To his surprise, the shuttle slowed and steadied into an even smoother circle than he'd managed to create when he was concentrating on it. Sulu sent the cloaked aircraft skimming around the first of the towers, staying well clear of open windows and crenulated walls where guards might be stationed. The far side of the fortress held something he didn't remember seeing before—a wide, enclosed courtyard jostling with military vehicles. Each one was surrounded by moving figures whose broad backs glittered green in the morning sun as they loaded pallets stacked high with supplies and piles of gleaming cylinders that must be weapons.

"The invasion forces you were talking about?"

Sulu asked Chekov as they glided over the sprawling supply yards.

"Yes." Chekov must have been counting in Russian under his breath. Sulu's helmet speaker picked up only an occasional mutter of "...*chetiresta vocyemnadset, chetiresta dyevyenadset, dyerto*..." before the older man said, "There's almost twice as many vehicles here as there were the day before yesterday. They must be pulling their forces in from all across this quadrant."

"That's good," said Sulu. "When we destroy the gate, more of their forces will be trapped here." For some reason, that comment struck Chekov into an extended silence, just the way Sulu's first use of "sir" had. "What's so funny now?" Sulu asked.

"Nothing," said the emotionless voice in his ear. "It's just that I keep forgetting you really *are* him, only younger. He said exactly the same thing when we first saw this place."

A shiver crawled up Sulu's spine. In his attempt to ignore it, he shoved his hands a little too deeply into the Gorn manipulative hollows and the shuttle surged across the terrace with a burst of speed he hadn't exactly intended to give it. Sulu cursed and pulled it back to a gentle glide, but not before he saw some scaled faces glance upward from their equipment-loading. With any luck, they'd put that puff of breeze down to the last of the sunrise storm.

"Hard aport," Chekov snapped. "Get us out over the forest, as low as you can."

Sulu had served long enough on the *Enterprise* to

know when he should obey first and ask questions later. Restraining the urge to hurry, he swung the shuttle across the crenulated edge of the Gorn fortifications and settled it down into the rain-wet fronds of a towering stand of tree ferns, just deep enough to let their visual deception screens blend in with the swaying greenery while leaving them a clear view of the massed Gorn forces. "Do you really think they noticed us?" he asked then, at last.

"No," Chekov said, surprising him. "But even if they shoot up a spray of energy disruptors just for the hell of it, they would knock us right out of the sky. It's not worth the risk." He paused a moment, then added with a thin wisp of something that might almost have been whimsical humor in his voice, "Mr. Sulu, could you turn the shuttle so I can see, too?"

"Sorry, sir." Sulu adjusted the shuttle's position with an ungainly lurch of its engines. It settled back down at ninety degrees to its former position, allowing both him and Chekov to gaze out from the wider side of the cockpit dome.

From here, they couldn't see the equipment loading terrace anymore, but they had a good view of the fortress's outer rim instead. The crenulated wall was almost obscured along this side by a vast tent city that had been erected in the clearing beyond. The tents were arranged with unmistakably military precision, color-coded from practical shades of green to drab grayish-black, then, on the outside the bright clashing reds, oranges, and purples that Sulu recognized as the colors of the great Klingon fighting houses. Knots of massive, green-scaled reptilian bodies clustered near the greenish tents. From their size and the immense sweep of their predatory jaws, Sulu assumed those were the Gorn. The few Klingons he saw among them wore elaborate armor and tied their hair in wilder, more barbaric fashion than the taut Klingon space officers he had met on stations in the Alpha Quadrant. But the distant figures Sulu stared at the longest were the unknown aliens he saw sitting on the ground near the dull black tents. They were the most humanoid of the three, with smooth faces and slender, tall bodies. A squinting look at their pale faces showed Sulu an eerily familiar combination of upward slanting eyebrows and pointed ears.

"Are those Vulcans?" he demanded incredulously.

"What?" Sulu felt their helmets scrape as the older man followed the direction of his gaze. "No, those aren't Vulcans. They're Romulans."

"Really? That's what Romulans look like?" Sulu tried to stand on tiptoe to see better and nearly lost his balance on his ungainly stilts. He steadied himself, then settled the Gorn shuttle back into the tree ferns. "Why do they look so much like Vulcans?"

"Because they're sibling races, originally evolved on the same planet." Chekov's voice had turned very thoughtful. "This is interesting. You don't usually see Romulans in Gorn first-strike battalions."

"Why not?"

"Slave race," the older man said succinctly. "The

Gorn crushed the Romulan Empire before they attacked the Federation because they wanted their ships and cloaking technology. The Romulans work for the Gorn at gunpoint, and they're often brought in to help run the bureaucracy on occupied planets. But I've never seen the Gorn trust them to help lead an invasion before."

Sulu frowned, remembering what Chekov had said when he'd first described the situation here. "You said they might be massing for an invasion of one of the major inner planets. If they were planning to invade Vulcan—"

"Then it would make sense to bring Romulans in the first assault wave," Chekov agreed. "Neither the Gorn nor the Klingons can match Vulcans when it comes to strategy and tactics, but Romulans can think the same way as their cousins." He startled Sulu with a sudden smack against his shoulder. "You know, you were right. It *was* worth coming out to reconnoiter the fortress one more time. Take us back."

"Back?" Sulu said blankly, and glanced back over his shoulder at Chekov. "Back where?"

"Back to your wrecked shuttle." Chekov's mouth, held in place by its mask of old scars, never changed expression, but there was an air of fierce anticipation in his squared shoulders and out-thrust chin. His dark eyes gleamed with an expression that caught Sulu by surprise: not just grim amusement, but what looked almost like delight. "We're going to salvage that magnetically shielded warp core of yours and bring it back here. It will do a hundred times more damage than a pulse bomb, especially if we can set it to implode inside of the portal."

"But how are we going to *get* it inside the portal?" Sulu demanded. "Do you know how much a warp core weighs?"

"A lot," the Russian admitted. "Do you know how many Romulan slaves it takes to carry one?"

"No."

"Me, either," Chekov said. "So we're just going to keep on freeing them until we find out."

The transportation alcove on the Janus Gate device looked less like a console and more like a piece of abstract alien sculpture. Chekov stepped gingerly into the curve of its embrace, trying to decide how to orient himself to its incomprehensible features. He could make very little sense in its conflicting lines and contours. Certain surfaces pointed upward, others angled down toward the floor, but he wasn't fooled into thinking this told him anything about what the original architects considered "up" and "down." Even the appendages Sulu had so casually pronounced handgrips looked unsuited to anything Chekov recognized as a hand, much less anything he would have called gripping.

"Place your hands on the device, please."

Chekov nodded and took a deep breath. He'd just promised Smith that the cold in the main chamber wouldn't bother him, that a lifetime of Moscow winters had made him impervious to anything above absolute zero. But he was shivering as he laced his hands around the Janus Gate's contact bars.

A vibration so slight it might have been the racing of a small animal's heart fluttered against his palms. The device wasn't cold like the rest of the chamber—it was blood-warm and yielding, almost like touching his own flesh.

"Using the readings we obtained from Captain Sulu's attempted transport, I shall endeavor to place you in the appropriate time frame." Spock made eye contact with him across the device's blue-flame heart. The weird light painted the Vulcan's face an eerie, dark gray. "However, I would suggest you describe what you see before we complete transport in order to verify the coordinates."

Chekov heard Sulu laugh from somewhere out in the dark chamber behind him. "It wouldn't help much if we both ended up on the *Kerzhat*." He didn't know how the captain could sound so relaxed.

"I understand." Chekov nodded again, swallowing hard in a throat that was suddenly painfully dry. "What happens if I let go?"

Spock lifted a curious eyebrow, apparently considering the possibility for the first time. "Logic suggests that either you will be severed from the device and our contact with your crisis point temporarily lost, or your physical form will be dispersed across the subspace rift into infinity."

Chekov was beginning to suspect that it was best

to enter into such heroics with as little information as possible.

"Don't let go," Sulu suggested dryly.

A net of electric blue light swarmed over his hands, and Spock's voice said from a very great distance, "I am engaging the time controls."

Lightning—silent, bright, actinic—seemed to vaporize the frost-blackened chamber around him. In its place, a sky so pale it was almost white, mirrored by an expanse of pristine snow and low, ice-covered houses.

"There's snow…" Ghostly sensations distracted him, making it hard to concentrate enough to report on what he saw. The sound of the wind as it cut between the houses. The prickle of snow against his unprotected cheek. "…I hear dogs…" And the syncopated calls of black-headed geese somewhere beyond his view. Chekov couldn't decide if this specific moment was familiar, or just representative of all his accumulated memories of the world he grew up in as a boy.

"That can't be right." Sulu's voice sounded startlingly real and nearby. "We're in a montane forest on Basaraba—we've never been in a snowy environment there. And I've never heard dogs or anything like them."

"Wait…" Chekov felt them rushing up from behind just before they burst into view under him—almost through him. A team of lean, rough-coated dogs towing a sledge, with a driver so young and out of control that he'd already lost one glove and the hood of his gray fur parka. The memory came back to him quite suddenly, and Chekov smiled at his own youthful indiscretion. "No, this is Earth—"

On the other side of the temporal rift, the sled cracked violently against something under the ice, leaped a startling height into the air, then crashed back to ground on its side. Unconcerned with the boy still dragging behind them, the dogs kept running with their tails flailing banner-high over their backs.

"—I'm twelve. I fell from a dogsled and was dragged—" He came nowhere near dying, but it was the first time in his life when he'd been honestly convinced he was about to be killed. If not by the dogs, then by their owner when he found out that Andrei Chekov's precocious son had "borrowed" his team without asking.

"Interesting." Chekov found it hard to believe that Spock found anything intriguing about his misspent youth. The Vulcan proved him right by adding a moment later, "Apparently the time placement controls are more individual than they first appeared."

"It sounds like you're about thirty-seven years off," Sulu volunteered.

Uhura said, "The device says, '*Major crisis point located within fifty-three [word unknown] units of time.*' "

Back in the transport chamber, years away from the boy who finally managed to extricate himself from the sled's rigging and roll to a stop behind the disappearing dogs, Sulu remarked irritably, "It would help to know what 'units of time' the device was using."

"Indeed it would, Mr. Sulu. Unfortunately, we have only limited data with which to work. Mr. Chekov?"

He felt funny answering aloud, as though the distant past version of himself would overhear and turn to look. "Sir?"

"I have located another crisis point. Are you ready?"

"Yes, sir. Go ahead."

The lightning flashed again, erasing the Russian countryside with a cobalt expanse of frigid nothing. He gasped at the sense memory of water flooding into his lungs.

"Mr. Chekov...?"

"It's the cave." He tried not to cough, but found it hard to separate himself from the remembered horror of struggling to find the surface, gasping for air only to flood himself with water so cold it stopped his heart. *"This* cave, earlier, when I...drowned. I'm not directly on top of myself, though. I'm about..." He tried to sense his own presence, vaguely felt the touch of a lifeless limb as it sank toward an unseen bottom. "...about a meter and a half away."

Darkness crashed aside, the faint blue light of the cave suddenly blinding him. Chekov took a deep, grateful breath of the chilly air as across the device from him Uhura reported, " *'Major crisis point located within fifteen [word unknown] units of time.'* "

Spock nodded, but didn't look up from his manipulation of the device. "Thank you, Ensign. Your input is helpful in fine-tuning the device's settings."

Chekov nodded mutely, not trusting himself with words.

The first crisis point had been easy—he'd survived it the first time, he remembered surviving it, and the memory had actually softened into a humorous story with a few years' distance. But the drowning—near-drowning?—left him feeling shaky and sick to his stomach. He barely remembered hitting the water, had no memory at all of being fished out and revived, thanks to the Janus Gate having switched him for a healthier version of himself. So which Chekov had he felt struggling in the dark water beside him? The one who had replaced him an instant before his own death? Himself just before the device switched him out the first time? Some other Chekov, in some other timeline, who didn't earn a second chance because Spock pulled this Chekov back without allowing a transfer?

He scrubbed at his eyes, trying to erase the feeling of cold water against his skin. It was hard enough to think about surviving a brush with death—he didn't like having to worry about whether all the various alternate versions of himself also survived.

"Engaging time controls."

Chekov hurried to wrap his hands around the contact bars. The cerulean flash—then the burnt-orange stain of emergency lighting—the stinging metallic stench of ozone and melted plastic—

Because it seemed important, he said immediately, "I don't recognize where I am." With that admission came a weird, illicit thrill. He was peering into his own future.

Sulu's voice again, unlocatable in the unfamiliar surroundings. "I guess the third time's the charm."

He didn't feel particularly charmed. Something like a hideous reverse déjà vu pushed his heart into the base of his throat. "It looks like I'm on a spaceship…or a station…." Duranium walls, with English writing barely visible in the spastic play of shadow and light.

"Can you see any kind of identifier?" He couldn't tell who asked him that.

His view slewed abruptly, away from the writing, toward a shattered doorway and the smoke-filled corridor beyond it. Chekov realized with a shock that he was almost completely overlaid on himself. A ghost painted into a dream world. Except in his dreams it was usually the sensations which were fierce and vivid, the visuals muddy and hard to recall.

"There was writing on one of the walls…give me a minute…."

He tried to will himself to turn. Instead, his future self glanced down, where an erratic smatter of bloody footprints hinted at a gruesome dance of combat and retreat. He caught a glimpse of his own hand, and a pistol-shaped weapon he didn't recognize.

"…There's been some kind of battle…."

A horrible sensation exploded through him from behind. He gasped, felt himself—one of his selves—arch away from a nerve-flaying anguish that almost rocked him out of his body. Then he was suddenly on his back, pinned to the ground by a force so powerful he swore it had drilled right through him and grabbed hold of his spine—

"Mr. Chekov, please report—"

—then the stinking mouthful of teeth so close to his face he could feel the ivory rasp against his cheek, and he realized the monster was speaking to him—a sibilant hiss that some part of him recognized as words even though he didn't understand. Without willing it, without thinking, he bucked beneath the thing's crushing weight and spat into its iridescent face—

"Mr. Spock, shut it off!"

—and a great clawed thumb curved along the line of his cheekbone and pushed into his eye—

"Shut it off before he lets go of the console!"

Chekov sat down hard on the floor of the Janus chamber, every nerve in his body still singing with the memory of the thing's bulk on top of him, its breath against his face. Curling forward, head between his knees, he clapped one hand over his still-tearing right eye and retched dryly into the other.

McCoy's head appeared around the edge of the conduit entrance. "Everything all right in there?" he called, alarm evident in his tone.

Spock replied with his usual understated calm. "We are all accounted for, Doctor. Please stand by."

"Pavel...?" Sulu slid to his knees beside Chekov. He felt the captain's hands on his shoulders, refusing to let go even when the younger man's first instinct was to scuttle away from the contact. "Pavel, where were you? Tell me what happened."

"...I was..." Chekov forced himself to lift his head and focus on the device looming directly above them. He thought it would help fix him back in this present, but instead it just made everything he was feeling seem more dreamlike and surreal. "...I was captured..." Saying it out loud helped a little. "They talked to me—I don't know what they said, but..."

Sulu's hand tightened painfully on his shoulder, a spastic, involuntary reaction. Chekov turned to look at him, and the captain said, very quietly, "Then you spit on them, and they put out your eye."

He didn't want to think about how Sulu knew the details, so he only nodded.

Sulu twisted to call over his shoulder, "We're still off by about five years."

Spock nodded acknowledgment, reaching to make a series of adjustments to the device's controls.

Sulu turned back to Chekov with an expression so bleak it was painful. "The Gorn took you captive during the evacuation of Starbase Six. I still had sixty-five people to clear out of the lower decks, and it took me more than twelve hours to come back for you." He lifted Chekov's hand gently away from his eye, reassuring them both with that simple gesture that it was intact and still functioning. "We were able to replace the eye. And you never told them a damned thing."

Chekov looked into this stranger's face, and tried to imagine inspiring the loyalty he saw there in anyone, much less this battle-hardened veteran. "You came back for me?"

"I only wish I'd come back sooner."

But you came back. He knew what a Gorn was now, and knew that both the Janus Gate and his future self believed at that moment that he was certain to die. Even Chekov wouldn't have faulted Sulu for giving up hope on his friend and not going back to find him. But he'd gone back anyway.

Chekov pushed to his feet, grabbing at Sulu's outstretched arm for support when he found his legs still a little unsteady. "We must be close now." *And I'm not going to leave you abandoned in the future.* If only because of a future debt he hoped would never come into existence, he owed something to this man he barely even knew.

Taking hold of the console, he squared his shoulders and nodded across the device to Spock. "I'm sorry for the delay, sir. I'm ready."

The Vulcan took him at his word. "Very well. Engaging time controls...now."

A fierce chill swept over him that he didn't remember from the first near-transfers, then settled on his skin as a sheen of cold sweat. Nerves, Chekov realized. Fear, that was all.

That was all.

He looked up from where he'd fixed his eyes stubbornly on the contact bars, across the device's familiar blue flame and skeletal housing. Uhura and Spock bent so close together over the lieutenant's translation equipment that their heads almost touched, and even the Vulcan's normally unreadable face held an expression Chekov could only interpret as mild surprise.

Uhura glanced up as though suddenly realizing the others would be waiting to find out what happened. "The device isn't identifying any future crisis points."

Chekov frowned, unbelieving. "That was the last dangerous moment in my life?"

Sulu moved up next to him, his expression grim. "We've nearly been killed at least a dozen times in the five years since Chekov was captured by the Gorn. Try again, Spock."

The Vulcan was shaking his head, a brief, regretful motion. "I have already moved the time variation control through a space representing Mr. Chekov's maximum possible lifespan. There may be other possible crisis points before that last one, but there is nothing it can fix on after that."

"Maybe it's not just a moment near dying that the machine locks in on," Uhura said quietly. "Maybe it's the fear that comes from *knowing* you're about to die."

Chekov felt more than heard Sulu's slow sigh. "You could be right. After those twelve hours with the Gorn, it seemed like Chekov never really cared again whether he lived or died." He looked at the young ensign in frank apology. "Maybe if I'd gotten there sooner, I could have saved the whole man and not just the eye."

Disappointment and frustration twisted together in Chekov's heart. "So you can't use me? I can't go?"

"It would appear not," Spock said.

Placing her tricorder beside Spock on the console, Uhura stepped back from the operator's console and squared her shoulders in what she no doubt meant to be a gesture of confidence. But it was determination Chekov saw in her eyes, not necessarily bravery. "Well," she said simply, "I guess it's my turn after all."

Chapter Nine

"CAN I ASK YOU a question?" Sulu said between gasps. The combination of Basaraba's thin air, rain forest humidity, and his current fierce exertion made his ribs ache with the effort to take deeper breaths than were physically possible. He couldn't see Chekov, but the other man's voice sounded equally labored.

"What?"

"Did the other version of me take your suggestions very often?"

There was a moment of silence, then the Russian's scarred face lifted just far enough over the silver curve of the shielded warp core to glare at him. "Yes, he did. All the time. Why?"

"Because it doesn't seem like you worry a lot about feasibility when you think up ideas like this."

Sulu heaved again at the mahogany-tough rain forest branch he was using to try to lever the warp core out of its cradle. The power supply for the wrecked *Edwin Drake* wasn't physically very large, but its dense dilanthanum shell weighed more than an equivalent ball of solid lead. With the added weight of Scotty's magnetically charged cryosteel shielding on top, the core felt as heavy as a chunk of a neutron star. "Why didn't we free some Romulans *before* we came back here to get this?"

That got him a snort and a stronger than usual heave on the other side. "Because they would have stolen our Gorn shuttle out from under us and headed for one of their homeworlds," said the Russian. "I've got a six-centimeter wedge open on this side. I just need another three centimeters to slide the antigrav disk in."

Sulu bent over, trying to recharge his lungs with oxygen for a final attack. He didn't waste any of it talking until after he'd thrown all his weight onto his makeshift pry bar again. The wood creaked ominously, but it made the warp core shift by a noticeable amount. "Is that enough?"

"No." Chekov heaved again on his side of the core. "I just need one more centimeter. Come on, you're twenty years younger than I am!"

"And used to a lot more oxygen!" Indignation lent Sulu a strength he didn't really have, and he managed a fierce dig under the core that brought it lurching up out of its cradle. He heard Chekov slam the antigrav disk home beneath it, then curse as the silvery sphere began to sink again anyway. Even the powerful anti-grav lifter couldn't totally compensate for the core's immense weight. Sulu managed to keep it from settling back into its cradle, but his uneven branch slipped off its smooth surface a moment later and the warp core rattled the shuttle's engine deck with its fall. He heard a gasp that didn't sound like one of exertion, and swung around to the other side of the shuttle.

"Are you all right?"

"Sure." Chekov was nursing one hand inside the other, but there didn't seem to be any particular expression of pain on his scarred face. It wasn't until he reached out to steady the core as it began to slide down the shuttle's tilted deck that Sulu could see the way two of his fingers bent at an unnatural angle.

"No, you're not," he said sharply. "Your fingers are broken!"

The older man grunted, as if that was a trivial detail. "Then it's a good thing I taught you how to fly the Gorn shuttle, isn't it," he said, with one of his mirthless cracks of laughter. "Come on, let's get this thing loaded."

Sulu blinked at him, concern slowly fading into a familiar chill of unreality and horror. This future in which broken bones were barely worth noticing and lives were sacrificed with grim satisfaction rather than sadness was one he suddenly wished he would never have to live through. Perhaps if he died today in Tesseract Fortress, Sulu thought, he could make that wish come true and save himself twenty years of agony and struggle.

In silence, he shouldered his part of the now manageable load of warp core and helped Chekov carry it out to the waiting Gorn shuttle. The smooth surface of the parabolic wing almost defeated them, but the Russian scrambled up into the cockpit and leaned out to lock wrists with Sulu as the younger man braced the weight of the core against his chest and shoulders. With a few fierce heaves that must have made his broken fingers stab with pain, Chekov hauled Sulu and the warp core together up the wing. They rested for a moment with the silver sphere balanced precariously on the cockpit rim, then Sulu swung himself beside the Russian and they lowered it down to the floor together. Not a word was spoken the entire time.

"The weight's too far aft for flight stability," was all Chekov said when he'd finally regained a little of his breath. "You'll have to stand on top of it."

Sulu nodded and slid the warp core as far forward as he could, then tried to balance himself on top of its smooth mag-steel cover. Coated with rotting leaf litter and buffalo dung, his boots slipped off as soon as he released his grip on the cockpit rim and tried to reach for the flight controls. "This isn't going to work."

"Yes," Chekov said flatly, "it is." He hauled himself up out of the Gorn shuttle, then climbed back a few moments later with their rain forest sticks clutched in his good hand. He wedged them between the sides of the Gorn shuttle, jamming the ends into the exposed structural supports of the wings and lashing them together with a length of self-sealing cable. "Try standing on that."

Sulu stepped gingerly up onto the makeshift platform, and felt it bow beneath his weight until it was stopped by the warp core. "It might hold me," he said dubiously. "But if the core slides out from underneath, the whole thing will snap."

"I won't let it slide out." Chekov sat down behind him, pulling on his sound-damping helmet and bracing his own body across the shuttle's hold to box in the core. He took a moment to jerk both fingers into alignment again with a wet *crack!* that made Sulu grimace, then said simply, "Come on, let's go."

Sulu pulled his own helmet on and yanked the cockpit cover closed overhead, then slid his hands into the hollow flight controls. The pressure-sensitive interior felt oddly damp against his skin, although he couldn't be sure if that was because it had collected some of the rain forest's humidity or because of his own clammy sweat. He didn't doubt that Chekov would do his best to keep the *Drake*'s warp core from shifting beneath him, but a lot would depend on how smoothly Sulu managed to fly this overpowered shuttle. With a deep breath, he pressed his fingers down into the right sockets and lifted off with an absolutely vertical surge. He let the shuttle's momentum take it as high as it would go before he added any forward thrust, allowing gravity to smooth the shuttle's transition from vertical to horizontal motion.

They were halfway back to Tesseract Keep before Chekov spoke again. "He modified them sometimes," he said abruptly.

Sulu spared a puzzled glance down at the older man, sitting with his shoulders rigid and braced against the lurching weight of the loose warp core and his broken hand cradled in his lap. "Modified what?"

"My ideas. Captain Sulu usually modified them, to make sure they would work. How close are we to the fortress?"

The abrupt change of subject warned Sulu not to make an issue of Chekov's awkward confession. "About a kilometer."

"Stay outside the perimeter wall," Chekov ordered, then grunted with the effort of keeping the warp core steady as Sulu swung the cloaked shuttle into a tight arc to avoid the Gorn defenses. "Find a place to land as close to the gray tents as you can."

Sulu scanned across the army encampment. "How about right in the middle of them?"

"What?" Chekov looked as if he was going to scramble to his feet, but at the last minute remembered that he couldn't leave his position. "How can there be enough room to land there? Those tents were packed in like herring."

"Not anymore." Sulu guided the shuttle in a slow, quiet arc over the encampment. There were almost no Klingons in sight now, and many fewer Romulans. "It looks like they've already started shipping the troops out. About half the Romulan tents are gone."

"Damn." Chekov was silent for a moment, then glanced up toward him with an odd, probing look in his dark eyes. "Were you really serious about landing right in the middle of them?"

"Yes," said Sulu.

"You know we would risk getting caught right away, if there's a Gorn or Klingon in sight when we open the shuttle."

"Yes."

He could see the Russian's lips move as if he had whistled, although his helmet communicator didn't transmit the sound. "You really haven't changed that much," he said. "All right. Take us down, Lieutenant Sulu."

Sulu already had the shuttle hovering near the spot he'd picked—a stretch of open stone near the crenulated wall of the wide mustering terrace, where they could make a quick dive over the edge if their plan failed and they had to escape. He cut the horizontal thrust to zero and let the vertical thrust slowly die away, trying for a graceful landing to match the rest of his smooth flight. The extra weight of the *Drake*'s warp core spoiled that by dragging the shuttle down much harder than he'd predicted. They landed with a rattling thump that must have been audible far across Tesseract Fortress's stone terrace, perhaps even all the way to the guardian towers that now loomed on the horizon.

Sulu didn't waste time apologizing. Even before the roar of the shuttle's engines died away, he threw the cockpit cover open and reached down to haul Chekov up toward the opening. The older man accepted the boost without a qualm, grabbing onto the edge with his good hand, then vaulting over it without hesitation. Sulu followed a second later.

As quickly as they had moved, it still hadn't been quick enough. They landed in the midst of a circle of weapons, and behind each gleaming metallic barrel was a lean, angular face taking aim with unemotional efficiency. Sulu felt a disorienting wave of disbelief—it was like facing an execution squad of multiple Spocks—but he drew himself up and made his expression as austere as he could, to match theirs. After one swift glance around to make sure there weren't any Gorn or Klingon supervisors in sight, Chekov did the same.

So far, the first part of their attack plan had worked. They had found one of the self-governed bands of Romulan slaves who were trusted to work without an overseer. Now, Sulu thought wryly, all they had to do was convince these quasi-independent alien fighters to cast their lot in with two bedraggled humans instead of the entire Gorn empire. He was glad that it was Chekov's job to do the talking.

"Humans," said one Romulan calmly. It didn't seem to be an exclamation of surprise or anger as much as a term of address. "How would you prefer to die?"

"Productively," said Chekov. "By killing as many Gorn as we can and taking their portal hub out with us."

That sent a response rippling through the circle of dark-uniformed Romulans, but it looked to Sulu like a wave of disbelief. Still, they made no move to shoot them or march them along to prison, and no green-scaled figures seemed to be converging on them from either the terrace or the towers. Their absence was explained a moment later when a deep thud echoed across the stone plaza, followed by the growl and clatter of heavy equipment being driven across the stones. The mobilization of the invasion force had saved them—among all the clangs and roars of moving equipment, the thud of their landing shuttle must have only seemed odd to the nearest troop of Romulans, who could see that the noise came from apparently empty air.

"How could you do that?" the leading Romulan asked. Her deep-creased face looked almost cruel with years of hard military service for the Gorn, but her dark eyes glittered eagerly as they bored into Chekov. "All your previous attacks on this place have failed."

"We have a warp core that can be set to implode inside the Gorn transport hub." Chekov scanned their faces, seeing the disbelief deepen, then said, "I know they scan for activated weapons as you enter the portal. But this warp core is shielded."

"How do we know you're telling the truth?" inquired another of the Romulans.

Chekov shrugged. "You can try scanning for yourself," he said. "Or just think back to yesterday, when that strange shuttle flew away from the Fortress after our last attack. The Gorn fired energy disruptors at it all the way from here to the outer ridge, but they never knocked out its warp core or its engines."

"I saw that." The Romulan leader silenced her subordinate with a swift gesture. "You took this shielded warp core from that vessel?"

"Yes." Chekov gestured at the shuttle behind them. "We can carry it, with the help of an antigrav lifter, but we'd never make it past the guards in front of the portal. We need you to take it in for us, disguised as part of your battle gear."

The Romulan leader's slitted eyes looked like chips of dark ice in her expressionless face. "While you stay safely outside?"

"Of course not," Chekov said, just as coldly. "How could we trust you to detonate it and not just turn it over to the Gorn? You'll take us inside with you."

"Disguised as Romulans?" asked the younger soldier.

"No," Chekov said crisply. "Disguised as your prisoners. All you need to do is think of some devious Romulan reason that makes it necessary for you to take us along to Vulcan."

"I think you can rely on us for that." The older female Romulan smiled, revealing a set of artificial titanium teeth. "Your plan is to implode the warp core inside the portal and blast apart the Gorn's transport system from the inside?"

"Yes," said Chekov. "Leaving them open to an attack by the Federation, and coincidentally helpless against any future Romulan uprising."

The Romulans exchanged glances of silent communication, and Sulu gritted his teeth as the agony of waiting for their answer dragged on. He was mentally debating whether their chances of making it back into the shuttle if the Romulans decided to fire were slim or none when the leader finally spoke again.

"This gamble seems worth taking, although the odds do not favor its success. We are willing to wager four lives on it. Agreed?"

"Agreed." Chekov stepped back and rapped his fist on apparently empty air. "I'll even throw in a shielded Gorn shuttle as part of the deal."

After watching Sulu and then young Chekov step up to take hold of the Janus Gate, Uhura had somehow thought it would be easier for her to do it. She was wrong.

It had been easy enough to pass the archaeological translator over to Carolyn Palamas and back away from the alien transporter's control panel. And it hadn't been too difficult to walk the perimeter line around to the other side of the ice-walled chamber, since her blue-tinted reflection seemed to walk along with her. Approaching the actual transport station was a little harder, but it was when she had to step into the strangely angled alcove and find a place for her hands on the alien gripping bars that Uhura found her breath stuck in her throat. Unlike the other two crewmen who had stood here, she had seen this alien blue light sweep out into the chamber and suck people into its time-crossing rifts. Although intellectually she knew she was in no danger right now, the looming possibility that Spock would soon be depressing the transport bar and removing her from this timeline was far more terrifying than Uhura had expected.

"I'm right behind you," Sulu said quietly. He stood where he had for Chekov, in the pool of protection that seemed to extend out from her awkwardly shaped slot. "Just be sure to tell me what you're seeing. I'll let Spock know how much he has to adjust time to get you to Basaraba from there."

Uhura nodded, because right now she didn't trust her tight throat not to strangle any words she tried to say. She tightened her grip on the uncomfortably slanted rods that connected her to the Janus Gate, then forced herself to look straight out into its flickering, dark blue heart. For some reason, seeing Spock gazing back at her with the same imperturbable expression that he usually wore on the deck of the *Enterprise* steadied her nerves and gave her the ability to speak again.

"Ready, Lieutenant?"

"Yes, sir." Uhura concentrated on meeting his gaze and not on watching the liquid streaks of fire climbing the arms of the transporter, then spiraling farther and farther up the bars she was gripping. There was a moment that felt like a strike of unseen lightning, bone-deep but skin-tingling at the same time. She opened her mouth to ask Sulu if this was how it had felt for him, but before she could do that, the ice-sheathed chamber seemed to suddenly leap away from her. It was replaced, after a moment of whirling nothingness, by what looked like the empty interior of a space station. Uhura could see stars glittering through several porthole windows, and what looked like reflected moonlight slanting in from behind her, but there seemed to be no lights other than that. She frowned, glancing around to try to locate something identifiable.

"I'm in a space station. It's dark, maybe unpowered." She tried to take a step forward to get a better view, but she didn't seem able to control her movements in this reality. "That's all I can see."

"Does it look like a Starfleet station?" Sulu asked, seemingly in her ear.

"I think so, but I don't see anything to identify it with."

"I am adjusting the distance control," said Spock's disembodied voice. There was another disorienting whirl, and now Uhura was standing in a dark shuttlebay, looking out through a hull breach at a wrecked starship as it drifted closer. She felt her throat contract instinctively, even though she knew the hard vacuum here couldn't reach her back on Tlaoli. "What do you see?"

"A starship, the *Alexander Jackson,* wrecked and heading for the station."

"That's the Gamma M14 station right before we abandoned it to the Gorn," Sulu said. "Spock, you need to move about eight more years into the future."

"Very well."

Uhura got a brief glimpse of blue light glittering off ice, then everything whirled around her again and condensed into a sandy desert landscape, blasted by a sun much stronger than anything she'd experienced in her time on the *Enterprise.* She told Sulu and heard him sigh. "Almost to Basaraba," he told Spock. "That's Chetay, the planet we were fighting on just before we found the Gorn portal. We nearly died of radiation poisoning there."

"Allow me to make a slight adjustment..."

The desert dissolved and was replaced by a stone-walled courtyard filled with the drifting smoke of a recent explosion. Uhura couldn't be sure, because her other senses seemed so muffled compared to sight, but she thought she could hear the sound of distant weapons fire in the sky. She caught a glimpse of a dark figure sprawled and broken on the stones, and looked away quickly. "I'm in some kind of courtyard, filled with smoke. I think someone's firing at a shuttle overhead, but I can't see because of all the smoke."

"That's Basaraba!" Sulu's voice had taken on an urgent sound that made Uhura's own pulse start to pound. "Spock, can you adjust the distance to get her past the Gorn defenses?"

"I believe so." There was another, shorter instant of disorientation, then Uhura found herself standing in the shadow of a stone archway, a tower looming overhead. The dark metal door ahead of her was closed, and she could see barrels of several weapons pointing out of slits in the stone beside it. "How is that?"

"Not good," Uhura said urgently. "The gates are locked and guarded. I think someone might have seen you, Sulu, when you were here before. It looks like they're waiting for us."

"Damn." She couldn't see him, but she could hear the sizzling frustration in his voice. "Is there anything else we can do to get there safely, Spock?"

"Perhaps," said the Vulcan. Uhura's stomach lurched as she felt another spinning moment of transition. Then she was back in the frigid air of Tlaoli's main cavern, staring across the flame of the Janus Gate at the ship's science officer. "I do not believe that varying the distance will provide the margin of safety you will need in order to stay long enough to locate Lieutenant Sulu. But as I become more familiar with these controls, I believe that perhaps we have more ability to vary the time of crisis substitution than I previously believed."

"What does that mean, Spock?" demanded McCoy's voice from the conduit outside the cave. "That you can pick and choose when to send Uhura to the future?"

"Not quite," said Spock. "I am still constrained by the overall timing of the crisis point for which we are aiming. However, since most events can be visualized as a bell curve of probability woven into the fabric of space-time, I can adjust the controls to place Lieutenant Uhura on either temporal cusp of the main crisis point. I may be able to place her in the time stream as much as a day before or after her death."

Uhura heard McCoy make a pained noise at the Vulcan's blunt words. "It wouldn't help her to get there early, before our version of Sulu arrives," the doctor pointed out. "And if she gets there a day late, he may already be gone."

"That would not be logical," Spock said. "Lieutenant Sulu should be able to reason that he must stay near the place where he first appeared, in order to facilitate a rescue from our side."

"And even if he doesn't," Sulu said quietly, "arriving a day late might let me get this pack full of explosives down into the heart of Tesseract Keep."

Spock lifted one eyebrow, as if that was not a major concern for him, but he didn't make an issue of it. "Are you willing to attempt going to Basaraba one more time, Lieutenant?" he asked Uhura.

"Yes," she said firmly. "And while *Captain* Sulu takes his explosives down to the portal hub, I'm still going to see if I can find *Lieutenant* Sulu."

"Very well." Spock bent over his controls, and once again Uhura watched quicksilver fire come streaking out from the Janus Gate toward her. That lightning-sharp shock shivered through her once again, and she found herself back in the original stone-walled courtyard where she'd seen her own limp body such a short while ago. It was empty now and filled with the slant of late-afternoon sunlight. Uhura could see thick rain forest trees overtopping the walls, their branches swaying in the breeze and dumping a glitter of collected raindrops down to the stone walls below. It looked oddly peaceful, after the mayhem of her last visit. Maybe a little too peaceful. Uhura had served in Starfleet long enough to know when something smelled like a trap.

"Spock, I'm not sure you should send us here," she said. "I can't put my finger on it, but there's something—"

There was another shock, a much deeper and more painful one, as if someone had dropped a metal lacework of electrically charged links across Uhura's body. She gasped and almost let go of the alien handgrips under the surge of pain.

"Spock, something's wrong," Sulu said urgently. "She's starting to shake, just like Chekov did... Uhura, don't let go!"

"I won't," she said and tried to see what was going on. Something interfered with her vision on Basaraba now—a shimmer like a heat-wave rose between her and the image of peaceful empty stones. Then, to Uhura's surprise, that image tilted and slid sideways, and slowly vanished behind her.

"Spock, are you changing the distance controls?" she demanded.

"Not at all. In fact," the Vulcan said, "I am attempting to bring you back again from viewing that point in the future. Unsuccessfully."

"*What?*" That was McCoy's indignant voice. "Spock, if this happened because you decided to push the limits on what this transporter could do—"

"I do not believe it is the timing of the transport which is the problem, Doctor," Spock said. "I am beginning to suspect Lieutenant Uhura has encountered some kind of force which is keeping her pinned into that future timeline, even in her half-materialized state."

Uhura took a deep breath, trying to ignore the constant prickle of what felt like small electric shocks across her skin. The sense of movement she felt now wasn't the disorienting whirl of the Janus Gate spinning her into a new time and place—it was the slow and lurching feeling you got when you were being carried by more than one person. With an effort, Uhura managed to slew her gaze around enough to look beneath her and see the bulging, dark-green shoulders of the four reptilian aliens who carried her in what looked like some kind of stretcher or poled support.

"I think Mr. Spock is right, Doctor," she said, wondering if only her teammates on Tlaoli could hear her or if she was making sounds on Basaraba, too. "From what I can see, it looks like I've been caught in some kind of force field. By the Gorn."

Tesseract Keep just felt *wrong*.

Sulu had never thought of himself as a man with a vivid imagination. Piloting a spaceship like the *Enterprise* required steady nerves and quick reflexes, but a talent for envisioning all the possible things that could go wrong would have been a hindrance rather than a help. Sulu's usual restrained demeanor reflected his calm temperament—one of the reasons his wild impersonation of D'Artagnan at Psi 2000 had been so mortifying.

He had expected Tesseract Keep to be intimidating and it was. Hewn of dark stone outside, barely lit inside and swamp-hot with the odor of many reptilian bodies, the Gorn fortress constantly vibrated with a powerful subsonic pulse as its transport hub worked deep underground. What Sulu hadn't counted on was the feeling that swept over him as soon as their Romulan "guards" marched him and Chekov at gunpoint through the stone entrance arch: that there was something so fundamentally flawed about this place that it shouldn't even exist.

"Chekov, what's going on here? Is this place built over some kind of natural dimensional rift?"

The Russian slanted him an unreadable look. "If I knew that," he said, lips barely moving beneath his stiff, scarred cheeks, "I'd know a lot more about how to—"

"*Silence.*" The Romulan behind Sulu dug his weapon deep enough into his ribs to make his breath vanish with a gasp of pain. "Prisoners do not speak."

It was a warning as much as a command, and Sulu tried to look properly discouraged. It wasn't all that difficult. There was still a long line of invasion troops to be cleared ahead of them before they even came close to the portal itself, much less were able to strip off the magnetic shielding of the *Drake*'s warp core and set the powerful antimatter heart to implode. For now, the warp core rode deep inside a Romulan photon-mine battery, concealed among the equally silver hulls of their deactivated weapons. They'd passed through a heavy metallic arch that Sulu suspected was one of the Gorn weapons scanners, but several gates and inspection points still lay ahead of them.

A dark column of Romulans stretched before and behind, stolid as the crates of supplies and weapons into the fortress. Their status as enslaved soldiers was obvious. Unlike the Gorn and Klingons, no large pieces of battle equipment accompanied the Romulans, and none of their arms seemed to be more than standard projectile weapons. Massive reptilian forms prowled along the line, poking at random groups to keep them moving into the shadowy interior of the keep. Sulu had never seen a Gorn except from the air, and he tried to keep himself from staring too openly at the sauroid aliens. But their sheer size, their fierce predatory jaws, and the spurts of mist that drifted from their broad nostrils even in this warm and humid air awoke a sense of unreasoning and instinctive dread. He couldn't imagine fighting these creatures for twenty years; he couldn't imagine taking on one of them in a hand-to-hand fight as Chekov said Gary Mitchell had once done. It was hard enough just to keep shuffling along when one paused to stare at him, craning its enormous head down so close that he could smell the carnivore reek of its breath.

"What is this?"

A deep rumbling sound accompanied that voice, but it took Sulu a moment to realize that it was the actual sound of Gorn speech. The English words came from a translating device the alien held clutched in one of its clawed hands. Sulu kept his head bowed and tried to look oppressed, taking his cue from Chekov's sullen slouch beside him. They left it to the Romulan leader to answer. She had surprised Sulu by being the first Romulan to volunteer for this suicide mission. He just hoped she had thought up a sufficiently convincing story about his and Chekov's presence while they'd been waiting in line.

"Prisoners." She poked Chekov with her weapon, hard enough to elicit a curse. "We caught them trying to infiltrate our camp."

The Gorn swung his massive weapon down toward them, growling. "Human scum. They should be killed."

"Of course," said the Romulan, and Sulu tried to hide his involuntary jerk of surprise by turning it into a cower. "And they will be, once they come through the portal with us. No human ever survives that trip."

"Why bother taking them, then?"

Her dark eyes glittered fearlessly back at her slave master. "Because their dead bodies will have strategic value on the other side."

The Gorn snorted thick mist across them, although Sulu wasn't sure if that was an expression of doubt or frustration. "Explain this strategic value."

Instead of answering, the female Romulan stepped forward and yanked Sulu's head back by the hair, forcing him to slew around with a cry of pain. He found himself staring straight up into the Gorn's sulfur yellow eyes, and fought the impulse to close his own. By now, he had guessed where this was going. "Retinal identification patterns are used to confirm Starfleet security levels," the Romulan said. "We can use theirs to break into the Vulcan's military computers."

"These patterns survive death?"

"As a network of tiny capillary arteries," the Romulan said. "But they must be as fresh as possible. The Vulcan security scanners are undoubtedly programmed to detect postmortem decay."

There was a long, considering pause. Then, without another word, the Gorn swung around and stamped away into the shadows.

"Did we convince him?" Chekov muttered, drawing the words out so they sounded almost like a whimper.

"I do not know." The Romulan leader pushed him forward into the gap that had opened in line while they talked to their guard. "He may be going to consult with his superiors about this—but at least he did not make us step out of line."

"Yes." Chekov glanced sideways, then stumbled a little on the stone pavement and caught himself on Sulu's shoulder. Sulu felt the older man's fingers flex through cloth into skin and muscle, hard enough to make him wince, but he betrayed no sign that a warning had been given. He had already realized that the Romulan leader's explanation of their presence here had been just a little too plausible for comfort. And without words or gestures, he knew what the Russian was now telling him.

If they couldn't get the warp core to implode before the portal began to activate, they were going to have to wrest one of the Romulan's weapons away and make sure their retinal patterns didn't survive one instant longer than they did.

Chapter Ten

EVER SINCE SHE WAS a child, Uhura had hated to be picked up and carried. It probably had something to do with being the smallest child among many cousins, the one who always got slung onto an aunt's hip or an uncle's shoulder to make sure she wasn't left behind. The inability to prove herself the equal of her older cousins had been frustrating enough to spark a lifelong determination to stand on her own two feet whenever possible. The result was an instinctive surge of irritation rather than fear at the situation she found herself in now—unable to move or control her movements because she really wasn't present in this time stream, unable to retreat back to her actual body because of the force field the Gorn had thrown up around her. Not for the first time, Uhura wished the ancient inhabitants of

Tlaoli had never decided to bequeath their time-traveling technology to the races that came behind them.

Except for vision, Uhura's other senses continued to tell her that she hadn't really gone anywhere. She could still feel frigid air bite at her throat when she breathed too deeply, and her hands still ached with the intensity of her grip on the Janus Gate. And she could hear, with perfect clarity, the heated discussion raging in the ice cave about the various ways her teammates might be able to manipulate the time device to bring her safely back where she belonged. But to humans, vision was the supreme sense. Despite all of the evidence to the contrary, Uhura's mind still angrily protested the lurch and swing of her surroundings as the Gorn carried her down a long walled passageway from the courtyard where she'd materialized, out of the slanting sunlight and into the darker shadows of a structure she couldn't really see. The Gorn carried her imprisoning force field in such a way that Uhura could only see out the back of it, and so couldn't even tell Captain Sulu what part of the Gorn fortress she was approaching.

"Give me your phaser, Ensign," Sulu ordered Chekov grimly. "Spock, use the associative transport and send me through the connection that's holding Uhura fixed at that time—"

"I will endeavor to do so, Captain, as soon as this chamber is cleared," she heard Spock reply. Then, "Mr. Chekov, take a small party to the other end of this cave system, where the alien healing chamber is located. If we are successful in retrieving Lieutenant Sulu from the future, I believe that is where he is most likely to be sent. Contact us by communicator as soon as you observe activity of any kind." There was a pause while the shadows of the Gorn fortress deepened around Uhura. She wondered if her eyes would adjust to this phantom light change when in reality she was still gazing into the fiery heart of the Janus Gate. "Prepare yourself, Captain Sulu. I am engaging associative transport now."

Uhura glanced around her limited range of vision, but saw no sign of Sulu anywhere nearby. "Did the transport succeed?"

"No." There was a biting edge in the older pilot's voice that hadn't been there before. "What is it this time, Spock? My hand again?"

"I do not believe so." The Vulcan's deep voice sounded more tense than usual. "I believe the associative transport has failed for the same reason that I cannot reverse Lieutenant Uhura's viewing mode. The force field which the Gorn are using seems to interfere completely with our ability to enter and leave the time stream. In fact, I am beginning to suspect it was designed precisely with that purpose in mind."

"The Gorn don't travel through time." It sounded as if Sulu was frowning. "They only travel through space. Why would they have designed a force field like that?"

"I do not know," Spock said. "I can only speculate based on the effect it is having on the Janus Gate."

"So what do we do now, Spock?" McCoy demanded.

"Wait," Spock said simply. "And be prepared to take action if the chance arises. The fact that Lieutenant Uhura is being carried suggests the Gorn have some purpose in capturing her. If they lower the force field in an attempt to accomplish it, we should then be able to sever the connection and retrieve her immediately."

Sulu's voice sounded a little clearer, as if he had turned back toward her. "Can you see where they're taking you, Uhura?"

"No." She had been trying to slew herself around without taking her hands off the Janus Gate's stabilizing handgrips, but the transporter didn't seem to translate her physical position into a changed viewpoint on Basaraba. All she could tell was that dark stone walls were closing in around her, and the passage seemed to be starting to slant downhill. After a while, she started to get glimpses of other figures through the heat-shimmer of her prison. To her surprise, along with squads of armored Klingons and the reptilian giants she assumed were Gorn, long lines of what looked like dark-clad Vulcans filled the halls. She reported that to Sulu.

"Those are Romulans," the older man said. "They must be going along as part of the Gorn invasion force. That means they've probably decided to attack Vulcan. Earth will probably be next."

"We're starting down what looks like some kind of spiral ramp," Uhura reported. "It just keeps going down farther and farther. We keep passing more Klingons and more Romulans."

"They must be taking you to the portal!" Sulu said fiercely. "Spock, are you sure you can't send me through? I don't even care if I'm dead when I get there, as long as I can set these explosives to go off without me."

"I would accommodate you if I could, Captain," Spock said somberly. "I am not indifferent to a potential future invasion of Vulcan. But at this point—"

"Sulu!" Uhura heard herself cry out even as she strained to reach across time and space toward a face made pale by its distance. "Sulu, I see you!"

The subsonic pulse of the Gorn portal hub grew louder as they approached the heart of Tesseract Fortress. They had left the entrance level behind long ago, and were now winding their way down a ramp that looked more like the entrance to an enormous pit mine than an architectural element. With the part of his brain that still seemed able to observe and analyze, Sulu found himself wondering if this had originally been nothing more than a mine on an outworld colony until the Gorn had stumbled across some kind of natural dimensional rift that allowed them to create their interstellar transport system. He remembered the discussion of natural subspace anomalies that they'd had back on the bridge of the *Enterprise,* when they first realized that the wrecks of alien spaceships littered the surface of Tlaoli. Had that been only a day or so ago? It felt like another lifetime to Sulu now, one that he would never get to finish living.

"Heads up," Chekov muttered. The lights were so dim down here that they couldn't see much of the ramps above or below them, but a new sound had been added to the constant subsonic rumble of the portal hub. It was the slapping thud of Gorn footsteps, coming down the ramp much faster than the rest of the invasion troops. Sulu felt all the muscles of his back clench with the immense effort it took not to whirl around and betray himself as that rush of feet came closer. Were they about to be exposed as saboteurs, or yanked out of line for further questioning by the Gorn? Sulu felt his breath choke in his throat, arrested by dread and the overpowering muggy heat that rose from the depths of the mine below.

"We can fight our way in from here," growled the Romulan leader, and Sulu heard her release her weapon's safety catch. No alarms appeared to go off when she did, and he wondered if he should tear off the cover of the weapons chest and start stripping the warp core of its shielding now. His gaze met Chekov's in silent query, and the older man gave him back a gruff shake of his head. There was still a chance, a very slight chance, that this downward rush of Gorn had nothing to do with them. It would be unutterably stupid to expose themselves too early if that were the case.

Apparently the Romulan leader thought so, too. She allowed her three subordinates to arm their weapons after she did, but when they began to lift them to their shoulders and sight back along the ramp from which they came, she snapped, "Not yet!" The order came not a moment too soon—the youngest Romulan had just finished slinging his weapon back across his shoulder when the platoon of Gorn came charging along the slope of the ramp toward them. The ones in front carried their normal weapons, their heads out-thrust suspiciously as they ran. Farther back, a group of unarmed Gorn carried what looked like a gold-brocaded sedan chair on their broad shoulders, boxed and curtained as if an ancient Asian emperor was venturing beyond the walls of his palace. As they came closer, however, Sulu could see that the golden curtains around that box were made of crackling sheets of pure energy rather than cloth. It was a portable force field prison, he realized, and it looked more than big enough to accommodate two humans.

"Make way!" roared the foremost Gorn, one clawed hand smashing into the nearest Romulan and hurling him back against the wall. They'd been so involved in anticipating an attack that, unlike the other groups of waiting soldiers, they'd neglected to clear a path through their section of the ramp. Sulu started to reach for the chest holding the warp core, but Chekov grabbed him hard with his unbroken hand and dragged Sulu away before he could betray their nonprisoner status. The Romulan leader single-handedly swung the weapons container out of the Gorn's way while her subordinates ruthlessly swept the two humans toward the wall with the butts of their weapons. Despite the pain, Sulu had to admire the Romulans' quick thinking. Held like clubs now, the weapons could be reversed and used against the Gorn at a moment's notice.

But to Sulu's amazement, that notice never needed to be given. The Gorn platoon swept past them with only the slightest of scornful looks, obviously intent only on reaching the bottom of the portal ramp as quickly as possible. Sulu dragged in a ragged breath, feeling as if it was the first he'd taken in a while. He let the musky, Gorn-scented air out again in a muffled sigh of relief, and felt the rush of air that meant Chekov was doing the same thing beside him. The last of the Gorn swept past, carrying the glowing force field on their shoulders, and the last of Sulu's breath ripped out of his throat in a cry so strangled he barely heard it himself. He felt more than saw Chekov swing toward him worriedly, but his eyes never left the back wall of that descending prison cell, where a familiar dark-eyed face had for one unmistakable moment peered out and *seen* him.

"What's the matter?" Chekov hissed as the line of troops waiting along the ramp shuffled themselves back into order and began to descend again. "Are you all right?"

"Yes." Sulu could barely force that whisper through his locked-up throat. "I mean, no. Chekov, didn't you see who was *inside* that force field?"

"No," the Russian said. "Who was it?"

"It was Uhura." Sulu met Chekov's disbelieving stare with all the resolution and strength of will he possessed. From this point on, he knew, everything was changed. *"My* timeline's Uhura."

"Uhura, I'm right here."

She heard Sulu's voice close beside her, felt him touch her arm back in the ice caverns on Tlaoli, and shook her head so fiercely she could feel the cold air slashing across her cheeks.

"No, *our* Sulu! He's here! I saw him just behind me, waiting on the ramp."

"Waiting to go through the portal?" Sulu cursed. "He must have somehow gotten in touch with Chekov, and they must be trying to attack the Gorn hub—"

"He seemed to be with some Romulans," Uhura said. "I didn't see anyone else with him." She paused. "I can hear some kind of machine pounding now, it's getting louder as we go downhill. Now we're going through a big metal gate. It looks like it's closing behind us."

"That must be the entrance to the portal hub," Sulu said. "Are they going to try and take you through it? Spock, what would that do to Uhura's connection back to us?"

"I do not know." The Vulcan's voice sounded more taut than Uhura could ever remember having heard it before, which made her own pulse kick with fear. "There is a chance the multiple subspace fields will create enough interference to free her. There is also a chance it will cause the Janus Gate's transport wave to collapse."

Uhura decided she would rather not have known that. "I see a lot more Gorn," she said. "They're looking through the force field at me, and they seem—Mr. Spock, I think they seem scared. Why would they be scared of me?"

"Maybe it's because you're not entirely materialized," Sulu suggested, and Uhura heard McCoy snort in the distance.

"So they're afraid of ghosts?"

"What we *don't* know about the Gorn would take me longer to tell you than what we know," Sulu retorted. "Uhura, do you seem to be moving toward any kind of opening or gate?"

"No, but there's a really bright light shining on the other side of this force field. It seems to be getting stronger—*ouch!*" A painful shock hit her again, stronger and more intense this time, as if she had been thrust through an electrically charged sieve into tiny dissociated fragments. Uhura closed her eyes and concentrated on keeping her hands clenched on the supporting bars of the Janus Gate. She could hear alarmed voices rise around her and feel the cold sting of involuntary tears freezing against her cheeks, but both sensations felt oddly muted, as if her connection back to Tlaoli was fading. That thought frightened Uhura enough to jerk her eyes open again.

At first, all she saw was that the force field around her was gone. Before she could open her mouth to tell Spock, however, she noticed that the heat-shimmer effect had simply expanded outward, multiplying itself to such an extent that it distorted everything beyond it to a crystalline haze. Several dark green smudges—the Gorn?—stood on the other side. On this side, all Uhura saw was the black rock pavement on which she stood, and a completely anomalous upholstered chair. It looked as if it had once been covered in sumptuous gold brocade, but time had faded it to a shredded spiderweb of dull ocher rags over a strange wire frame filled with what looked like electronic circuitry. Uhura took a step closer to examine it, then realized that she had regained control of her perspective in this place, and swung around to see what was happening behind her.

A humanoid figure, so thin-boned and adolescent it was impossible to tell if it was male or female, regarded her muzzily across a stretch of empty stone. It wore a simple Grecian-style robe that might have once been white, but now looked as faded and ragged as the upholstered chair. Dark bruises splotched across the figure's alabaster skin, but its long braided hair gleamed in the bright golden light from the force field surrounding them. Bloodshot eyes the opaque milk green of a tropical swamp peered at Uhura for a long time before the chiseled lips parted to speak.

"How...nice. A visitor."

Uhura blinked in surprise. It seemed as if the alien had spoken to her in English, but how could that be? Her universal translator was still back on Tlaoli with the rest of her gear. She didn't think the sounds she heard so faintly here on Basaraba were even being transferred out into the ice cave for her teammates to hear, much less sent back to her in translated form.

"Who are you?" she asked the golden-haired form.

"My name..." There was a long pause as the milky green eyes turned oddly vacant and inward. "I don't...remember anymore. I had a name once."

Uhura lowered her voice a little, not wanting to stress this fragile, mysterious being. "Do you remember what you're doing here? Are you a prisoner?"

"Uhura." That was older Sulu's voice, quiet as a moth fluttering by her ear. "We can only hear your side of this conversation. Can you phrase your questions to tell us as much as possible about who you're talking to?"

"A *prisoner*." The alien gifted her with an angelic smile, as if it had been searching for that particular word for a long time and was delighted to have found it. "Yes, I am a prisoner. Of the Gorn."

"I am a prisoner of the Gorn, too," Uhura said. She tried to pack as much information as she could into her next question. "You look like a young adolescent of my species, but you are much taller. What race are you a member of?"

"I am..." There was another long and vacant pause, but this time Uhura could see a hint of deeper awareness struggling to bubble up beneath the glassy vagueness of its eyes. "I am...a Metron."

"A Metron." The word sounded familiar to Uhura, but it wasn't until she heard Sulu's strangled gasp back on Tlaoli that she remembered where she'd heard it before. This was a member of the powerful alien race that had mediated the original dispute between the humans and the Gorn! The race that had summarily cast the Gorn into exile from space by destroying all their starships along with their crews. "I thought the Gorn used to be *your* prisoners," she said, and heard Sulu's murmur of wordless approval at this line of questioning. "What happened?"

The alien shook its head, slowly, sadly, but it took a long time for it to form words that could express the emotion clouding its thin young face. "I was visiting here to...to look, to watch, to see—"

"You came here to monitor the Gorn?" Uhura asked when it seemed to stumble over another word it no longer remembered. The alien beamed at her again, its sadness drifting away like clouds dispersed by a morning sun.

"Yes. I *monitor.*" It pronounced that word the same way it had said "prisoner," like an old friend newly met after a long absence. "I monitor the Gorn. Yes."

Uhura wondered if it had already forgotten her original question. "Then how did the Gorn manage to take you prisoner? I thought the Metrons were a very powerful race."

"Powerful." A wash of pride seemed to clear a little of the mist from the Metron's eyes. "Yes, we are powerful. We exist in more dimensions than most races know. But on this world, the Gorn discovered a...a substance, an essence, an organic chemical..."

It was running out of vocabulary again, Uhura

guessed. By now, however, she was also beginning to guess what its problem was. "The Gorn discovered some kind of drug, here on Basaraba," she said clearly, so that both Sulu and Spock could hear. "A drug they used to make you helpless while they broke free of their prison."

"A *drug*." The Metron nodded, as if every new word she gave it added another fragment back to its intellect. "Yes, a drug. They give it to me always since then." A graceful sweep of one bruised hand indicated, for some odd reason, the threadbare chair. "And then this force field keeps most of me in it."

Uhura blinked at it again, wondering if that turn of phrase reflected the alien's drugged mind or some deeper reality. "The force field keeps *most* of you in?" she repeated, to let Sulu and Spock hear the Metron's odd expression, too. "Where is the rest of you?"

"Pulled away." Long slender fingers touched the bruises on its bare arms. "They cut, they separate, they take away..." The almost violent way it moved its hands suggested to Uhura the word that it might be searching for, although she didn't understand how that word would apply.

"The Gorn *amputate* parts of your body?" she ventured, and got the angelic smile that she now knew meant she had given the Metron not just the word but the entire mental concept for which it had been searching. As far as Uhura could see, nothing seemed to be missing from its humanoid frame, but she remembered what it had said about Metrons existing in more dimensions than other races. "Where do they take the parts of you they amputate?"

It was the Metron's turn to blink at her. "Wherever it is they want to go."

Uhura gasped, so deeply she could feel the frigid air back on Tlaoli drive a spike of pain deep into her chest. When she exhaled again, she tasted an odd tang at the back of her throat, bitter and musky at the same time. "*You* are the Gorn's transport system," she guessed, and heard Sulu's muffled cry of surprise. "They've kept you here, drugged and helpless, for all these years. And they've used you to create their bridges from world to world."

"Yes." The Metron closed its milky green eyes for a moment, then opened them again. They seemed just a little more brilliant when it did, as if a sheen of tears had slid across them. "I try to hurt them," it said, defensive as a child explaining an accident it had caused. "Every time I send them, I try to hurt them. Sometimes I think I kill a lot of them, but usually I don't."

Uhura swallowed past another wave of shock. The taste of bitter musk was growing stronger. "I think some of the ones you've killed were trying to fight the Gorn," she told the Metron, as gently as she could. "You didn't know that?"

"No." The slender alien frowned, and Uhura saw another fragment of intelligence slowly surface from the murk in its mind. "I mean, yes. Sometimes I feel them attack me, those ones who are not Gorn. I wish I could tell them not to. My existence is too strong, it crosses too many dimensions. Any weapon they use will only be turned back on themselves. You will see." Its opaque green eyes met hers, sadly. "You will see, when the ones entering the portal now try to explode the weapon they have brought with them."

Only five Romulan soldiers remained in line ahead of them, now. The powerful heartbeat of the Gorn portal hub had risen to a rhythmic thunder as they descended deeper into the pit below Tesseract Fortress. At the end of the line loomed a massive titanium door which opened just far enough to let in small groups of invasion forces along with their equipment. When it was open, Sulu could see the yellow-white flare of a larger force field beyond it, although he wasn't sure if that marked the edge of the portal itself or was just a protection against last-ditch attacks. He watched as two of their Romulan allies discreetly dug the *Drake*'s warp core out from its covering of photon bombs and left the lid of the weapons chest ajar. A moment later, Chekov eased back to stand beside that opening, slipping his good hand inside to begin loosening the magnetic cover from the warp core's dilanthanum shell. They wouldn't actually take the core itself out until they were sure they were past all of the Gorns' scanners, but this way they would have a head start on activating its implosion sequence once they were actually standing on the verge of the portal.

Time was running out, and Sulu still hadn't decided what to do about Uhura.

She *must* be on the other side of the titanium gate. Sulu had no evidence other than the matching golden color of the two force fields he had seen, but he felt an irrational sureness that he would see her once they had been admitted. *And then what?* he asked himself sharply. If she had been haplessly thrown here by the ancient Tlaoli time transporter, the same way he had been, then they were both at the mercy of the Gorn and nothing could change that. It would make no sense to abort their attack on the Gorn portal hub just to make sure Uhura was all right. Wouldn't the kindest thing he could do be to destroy them both right now in the clean, instantaneous annihilation of a runaway matter/antimatter reaction?

But what if Uhura *hadn't* been sent here haplessly? What if the *Enterprise* crew back on Tlaoli had figured out how these time transfers were happening, and were trying to bring Sulu back to his proper place and time? Would he ruin everything by going along with the original attack plan? Shouldn't he at least try to locate and talk to Uhura before he let Chekov trigger the sequence that would lead to warp core implosion?

The questions tangled in Sulu's mind, hopelessly obscured by the numbing thunder of the hub portal and the freezing awareness that time was running out. The titanium door swung wide again, filling the darkness with the refracted glow of the force field beyond it. Sulu watched the last five Romulans ahead of them haul their sledge full of battle supplies through that gap, then felt a blast of ovenlike heat roll out, along with a musky smell so strong he thought it couldn't just be from the body oils of the portal's Gorn watchmen.

"Chekov," he said, as the door slammed shut and left them staring at it across empty darkness. "As soon as we go in, I'm going to try to find Uhura."

"No." The Russian didn't bother to glare at him, but his voice conveyed his disapproval clearly enough without it. With no one in front to observe them and the tall figures of Romulans shielding them from behind, he had flipped open the lid of the weapons crate and was openly dissembling the warp core inside, although he left the magnetic shielding propped above it to keep any last weapons detectors from going off. "You won't have time. We have to activate the implosion reaction right away."

"But if she's here to help us—"

This time, Chekov did glare at him, a look so hard and ruthless that Sulu almost stepped back from it. "In twenty years, this is the closest we have come to stopping the Gorn invasion," he snarled. "If you screw it up by trying to find someone who is already dead, I will borrow one of these Romulan weapons and shoot you down myself."

It was not a joke, or an idle threat. Chekov meant it. Sulu stood silent for a long moment, holding the older man's stare. None of the Romulans moved or spoke, although Sulu noticed one of the younger ones hitched his weapon a little farther forward on his shoulder, as if to make it easier for the Russian to grab it if he needed to.

"I won't ask you not to start the warp core sequence," he said at last. "But that's *my* shielded warp core you're using to blow up this fortress. You wouldn't be here if it wasn't for me getting thrown out of my rightful place in time. The least you can do before you blow me up is let me find out if Uhura's here because she came for me."

Chekov opened his mouth, but the portal's titanium gate began to swing open before he could reply. The Romulans didn't wait to see if the two humans would resolve their argument—the female leader snapped down the magnetic shielding on the warp core while the other three hefted the crate by its handles and headed for the gate. They moved quickly enough that Chekov and Sulu had to hurl themselves into a dead run to keep up. For all his age and injuries, Chekov still beat Sulu to the opening. Sulu felt the hot metal of the gate slam against the back of his legs as he dove through the last of the gap.

Inside, the yellow-gold glow of the force field was so bright that, at first, Sulu couldn't see past it to the rest of the room. When he finally blinked away the dazzle, he was surprised to discover that the force field was not located at the center. There was a titanium-floored platform there instead, looking surprisingly similar to the main transporter platform of the *Enterprise*. Behind it was what looked like an immense power plant, blasting out a fierce, dry heat along with the thundering roar they had heard all the way down.

It wasn't clear what part the glowing force field played in this unusual transport system, but it was certainly the focus of attention for the Gorn who were present. They were gathered around it, conversing in barely audible and untranslated roars and grumbles. No one seemed to be paying much attention to the empty central platform.

The Romulans paused slightly on the threshold of the room, and Sulu thought he saw a speculative gleam enter the leader's eyes as she glanced back over her shoulder at him. For a chilling moment, he wondered if she was about to betray them to the Gorn for whatever strategic advantage it might gain her, and he cursed himself for arguing with Chekov and placing both of them too far away to grab for one of the Romulans' guns. But although the female's face creased in a remarkably cruel smile, she waved Chekov toward the platform along with the three subordinates who carried the weapons chest. The older man went without a backward glance.

The Romulan turned back toward Sulu, pointing her gun in his direction vaguely enough that he didn't think it was meant to be a threat. "They aren't watching like they usually do," she said. "But they will notice in a moment that we haven't gone through. Why don't you try to escape now?"

Sulu blinked at her for a moment, uncomprehending. Then he glanced at the others, who'd stopped

Chekov before he could step up onto the platform. The Russian knelt beside it instead, stripping off the warp core's magnetic shielding so he could finish activating its implosion sequence. The others closed in around him, blocking the Gorn's view of what he did.

"We need to buy them some time," he guessed. "You want to create a distraction."

"What I want," said the female Romulan implacably, "is for you to escape now."

Sulu glanced around the room, seeing no trace of either Uhura or the portable force field prison in which she'd been confined. No one had come back up the ramp again, so unless they had taken her through the portal itself, Uhura had to be in here somewhere. That meant some of the Gorn peering so intently into the larger force field had to be the ones who had carried her down.

Without warning, Sulu darted past the Romulan officer and toward the force field, trying to let his motion explode in a way that would draw the Gorn's eyes toward him so quickly that they wouldn't spare a glance for Chekov. With a hissing noise, the Romulan leader leaped after him. She let him get just close enough to the force field to see a tantalizing glimpse of shadowy figures inside, then tore him away and threw him down on the ground hard enough to make his breath whoosh out from his chest. Sulu scrambled to his feet, gasping, then hurled himself sharply backward to avoid her threatening advance.

Most of the Gorn still seemed to be engrossed in whatever they were watching, but two or three glanced up to see what was going on. The closest swung his massive weapon around with reflexive and deadly accuracy to aim at Sulu. With an equally fast reaction, the female Romulan vaulted between them and slammed Sulu flat to the ground with the butt of her own weapon. Sulu felt pain strafe up along the side of his ribs, and gritted his teeth against the sudden effort it took to breath. Broken ribs were a small price to pay for that near-miss. He knew he was lucky not to be dead.

"Human cretin," spat the Romulan. "Either way, you die."

Sulu turned his head against the floor, breathing shallowly to keep his ribs from screaming in pain, and tried to squint past the glare of the force field. All he could detect was that one shadow was much taller and thinner than the other. He couldn't tell if the smaller one was Uhura, but the portable force field cell they had brought her down here in lay tumbled on its side and unheeded next to the larger field's perimeter.

"Shoot him," rumbled the closest Gorn through his crude translating device. "If you take him through the portal, he will die soon anyway."

"Then why waste the energy?" The Romulan reached down and jerked Sulu to his feet, wrenching a groan of pain out of him despite his resolve not to cry out. "He's not worth—"

A shrill warning alarm cut across her voice. It was so familiar, and so reminiscent of his life back on the *Enterprise,* that Sulu felt his stomach lurch with loss instead of shock. A moment later, a computerized voice said in typical calm Starfleet style, "Warning. The antimatter containment field of this reactor has been breached. Evacuate the area immediately. Core implosion immanent."

Chapter Eleven

EVEN IF SHE HADN'T seen Sulu standing in the long line of Romulans, Uhura would have known immediately that the weapon the Metron spoke of must have been brought in by the last two humans on this planet. She felt her pulse begin to hammer in her throat again, and tried to swallow past the fear. If the Sulu here on Basaraba blew himself up before she could reach him now, she wasn't sure there would be another time to which the Janus Gate could send her where she could save him.

"Spock," she said urgently, not caring now if the Metron wondered who she was talking to, "Sulu and Chekov are bringing some kind of weapon into the portal right now. The Metron says it can't hurt it because it extends across too many dimensions. What should we do?"

She heard the other, older version of Sulu groan at the news, but the crisper voice she was waiting for didn't come. Uhura felt a faint, distant tingle run across her skin and wondered if the Vulcan was attempting to retrieve her through the Janus Gate. She held her breath as the tingle grew stronger, and the bitter musky taste in her mouth almost choked her. Uhura glanced around with sudden understanding, seeing a faint greenish mist coming out from the circuitry at the base of the tattered chair. The drug the Gorns were "always giving" to the Metron must be airborne, and it was coming in through the miniature transporter that had originally been hidden inside that chair! And if she could somehow taste it back on Basaraba, then she was here as more than just a ghostly visual image. There was at least a fractional amount of physical exchange going on.

"Sulu," she said softly, so as not to disturb Spock. "Can you smell anything in the air around me?"

There was a pause, then the older man said just as softly. "A tang, like hair and metal burning. Is that the drug?"

"Yes." Uhura glanced at the chair. "It's coming from a small transporter unit. The Gorn must need to keep it at a consistent level—I think it's been coming in all the time I've been here. If Spock could just take that small transporter unit away—"

"The force field is still interfering with my ability

to fully engage the Janus Gate," the Vulcan said, entering the discussion so calmly that Uhura suspected he had heard all of their muttered comments. The ice cave back on Tlaoli must be utterly silent. "But I believe I have enough control to try something else. Lieutenant Uhura, I must ask you to stand as close to the Metron as you possibly can."

Uhura didn't hesitate. Using her will as much as her not-quite-there body, she managed to fling herself across the space between her and the golden-haired alien who was just now parting its lips as if to question her. Even as she went, Uhura felt the tingling sensation grow to an unpleasant needling that made her skin prick into goose bumps of response.

"What are you doing?" The Metron stepped back when she approached, a slow alarm drifting into its opaque eyes. "You shouldn't touch me, it will throw you through the portal…"

Uhura stopped about a half-meter away, seeing that the alien had backed itself almost into the force field. "You have to let me stand close to you," she pleaded. "We're trying to free you."

"We?" The Metron peered around the empty stone floor as if it thought it had somehow missed seeing someone who was in here with them. "Who are *we?*"

"A group of humans from another place and time," Uhura said quickly. She wasn't sure how much time she had left to convince the Metron to trust her. And whatever Spock was planning to do, there was no way of knowing how long it would take for the Gorn's airborne drug to fade from the alien's multidimensional body. "I'm not really here completely...part of me is still back in the place I came from."

"I understand," said the Metron. "That is why they brought you here to me. They must have thought you were another of my race."

"We are going to try to free you," Uhura told it. "But for it to work, I *must* stand as close to you as I can."

The Metron's eyes seemed to grow just a little clearer. "Approach, then," it said, and held its arms out and back, as if holding back something unseen behind it. "I will try to keep from sending you anywhere."

Uhura took a deep breath, her lungs filling with an odd mixture of both frigid and musky air, and moved closer again to the Metron. As she did, the needling sensation across her skin grew even more intense, as if somehow her body was absorbing and reradiating the energy fields in conflict all around her. Uhura steeled herself to bear it, even when it seemed to sink down through her skin into the muscle and bone beneath and deepened from discomfort into actual pain. After a few seconds, she realized that the goose bumps on her skin were still there, however, and a moment later she realized why. The air around her was growing colder, much colder....Spock was using the Janus Gate's associative transport function to send all he could to Basaraba through her flickering connection. And what he was sending was Tlaoli's glacial but absolutely pure air.

The Metron stiffened and jerked its eyes closed. Uhura thought perhaps it was just trying to hold onto its strength, to hold back the cross-dimensional transfer into which it might involuntarily hurl her. But then the alien's eyes fluttered and opened to stare at her with an expression so intense it was almost awe.

Its eyes were a pure and glittering emerald.

"I am...whole." The Metron glanced down at its alabaster arms and one by one the bruises disappeared. "I am one again." It glanced across the room at the threadbare chair, and that abruptly disappeared as well, making the air crack like thunder as it rushed into the space that had been vacated. "And I *will* be free."

With a roar, the force field exploded outward around them, crumbling into diamond glitter and shrieking fragments of displaced energy. Uhura felt the pain burst away from her as that confining field disappeared. She staggered in the whirling aftermath, and heard Captain Sulu's voice shouting in her ear.

"Don't let go! Uhura, don't let go! We're going to try to bring you back!"

"Not yet!" She tightened her phantom, barely felt grip on the Janus Gate and spun around, looking for the Sulu she knew. A massive row of Gorn faced the Metron, their predatory jaws open in what might have been either startled gapes or angry snarls. The golden-haired alien gazed back at them contemptuously. Then, with a flick of its fingers, they were suddenly gone. The Metron turned toward the other figures standing in that chamber, and before Uhura could force words through her cold, dry lips, they vanished, as well.

"Wait!" Uhura cried out, and the Metron glanced across at her. Its emerald eyes were as clear now as a deep-green tropical sea. With the room empty, she could see that there were only two people left: one crouched protectively over what looked like a partially disassembled warp core, one crumpled and gasping with pain on the floor right in front of her. Uhura recognized his stained and sodden Starfleet tunic. "These are my allies! Let me take them back with me—"

"Very well," said the alien, calmly. One gesture swept the two men together and dumped them carelessly at Uhura's feet, then the Metron moved away, floating rather than walking across the chamber to examine the silver object gleaming at the foot of what looked like a huge transporter pad. "Ah...an antimatter power plant. Even better than a weapon...and its confinement shield is just about to breach—"

Uhura knelt down beside the men she had been gifted with, feeling another painful jolt as her not-quite materialized body made contact with them. "Spock, bring us home," she ordered. "Bring us home *now!*"

There was a momentary pause, then the whirling nothingness of time transfer seemed to surge in upon Uhura, this time manifesting itself as a powerful vortex whose core was her. The Gorn portal began to dissolve and spin itself away at the edges of that nothingness, but not before Uhura heard the sound of what must be Metron laughter, light and silvery like fairy bells heard in the distance. Then, distantly but clear as crystal, the sound of the alien's voice.

"What a lovely going-away present for my gracious hosts."

"Here they come!"

Chekov jolted awake with a gasp, snapping his head up off his arms and wondering for one brief, panicked instant where he was and why he was sleeping in the cold.

Then the distinctive smell of the cave's frozen travertine bit at his nostrils, and his eyes locked on the twin columns of swirling gold rapidly brightening out on the main floor. The details of the last two days swept over him like a splash of cold water—including the memory of Spock placing him in command of this little party when the Vulcan sent them up here to wait.

"Let's not get too excited." Zap Sanner's voice sounded closer than Smith's, but still rebounded through the column-filled chamber too wildly to locate. "We might have quite a wait ahead of us before the machine lets them out."

Chekov scrambled to his feet, half-blind in the dark despite the growing brightness of the columns, and called, "Mr. Smith, call Mr. Spock and report that we have activity." He hoped he didn't sound too sleepy or caught off guard.

Smith's answer gave him no clue. "Aye-aye, sir."

Despite the lengthy walk to the upper chamber and the lengthy period of inactivity he'd known was waiting for them there, Chekov had not for one moment considered that he would fall asleep while waiting for his crewmates to materialize. He'd been tense with excitement at his first (albeit tiny) command, and the adrenaline pumped into his system from his own brush with the future still had his stomach fluttering and his mouth too dry. He'd expected to pace back and forth in the dark, monitoring the others' locations around the chamber and keeping his hand close to his communicator in preparation for signaling Spock at the first sign of activity.

Instead, he was groggy from an uneasy sleep that hadn't been at all restful, patting blindly for his helmet among the rocks of the breakdown pile while smothering a fresh yawn against the palm of his hand.

The purring rasp of a carbide ignitor caught his attention, and he looked up just in time to see James Kirk's face appear in the darkness above a freshly lit helmet lamp.

"What are you doing here?"

"Your job, apparently." Kirk passed the lit helmet down to him, then scooped up his own from the rocks nearby and struck its light with a single practiced flick of his thumb. "Don't worry—you didn't miss anything."

Chekov stepped back to give the boy room to hop down to the floor, but didn't make any effort to hide the irritation on his face. Kirk ignored him with what could only be the ease of long practice. Clapping his helmet atop his head, Kirk asked, "Don't any of you guys keep regular hours? Everybody up top is snoozing, too."

Chekov kept his helmet in both hands, remembering what Uhura had said about the lights making it hard to identify faces. "We've all been on emergency status these last few days," he said, starting in the direction of Sanner's and Smith's collected lights. "That has a tendency to disrupt your schedule." *Which isn't an excuse for falling asleep on duty.* But he didn't admit that to his future commander.

Kirk's interest had already been drawn to other things. He waved toward the nearest bright gold column, his mouth tweaked into a grin of triumph. "Told you they glowed."

He had, although Chekov hadn't thought about that particular detail since then. Abruptly, he realized that the glowing Kirk had seen upon his arrival on Tlaoli was someone being healed inside one of these alien medical chambers. Someone who had been plucked from certain death at another point in the timeline and deposited here to be recycled. *Me,* Chekov thought with a little start. *Me, after the drowning. Me, just before I died.* He suddenly didn't feel at all sleepy anymore.

Sanner glanced up as they drew near. His eyebrows flew up almost under his helmet when he caught sight of Kirk. "How did you get down here?"

The boy held out the front of his mud-soaked shirt as though that made the answer obvious. "Through the sinkhole. You left all the ropes."

"I should never have taught you how to rappel," Sanner complained with a sigh.

The geologist's disapproval didn't appear to affect Kirk any more than Chekov's had. "So what is this?" the boy asked, studying the nearest glowing pillar. It had swelled almost too bright to look at directly, the humanoid figure inside blurred beyond recognition beneath layers of ancient flowstone. "Part of your alien transporter?"

"The arrival gate," Sanner said. "The machine puts you through these healing chambers before it lets you out into the room. At least, that's what we're pretty sure it does."

Kirk nodded, his eyes still taking in every detail of the strange device. When he finally glanced aside at Chekov, the ensign wasn't surprised to see an uncertain thoughtfulness hiding there. "This is your pilot coming home?"

Chekov nodded. "That's what we're hoping."

Kirk looked back at the machine. "So who's he bringing with him?"

Before Chekov could decide how to explain the situation they'd left behind in the ice cave, the nearest of the two columns dimmed to darkness and Sanner remarked, rather cheerfully, "It looks like we're about to find out."

Chekov put out one arm as a signal that they all stay together, even though no one had made any particular move to disperse. It just seemed like the sort of thing the party leader should make sure of. "Lieutenant?" Even as he called out, he realized that he didn't know which lieutenant he should be expecting to answer—Sulu or Uhura. After all, Spock must have figured out how to fully transport Uhura into the future long enough for her to retrieve Lieutenant Sulu. If not, how could anyone be arriving now? Suddenly afraid of leaping to an assumption that would only serve to make him look uncertain, he called, "This is Ensign Chekov. Mr. Spock sent us up here to meet you."

Kirk elbowed him silently, and Chekov followed the boy's nod to a dim spot of movement in the pillar-littered darkness. He strained to catch the first spark of reflection off a gold-braided sleeve, or the flash of Sulu's relieved smile as the lieutenant neared the halo of their combined lamplight. Instead, the figure which approached them—unhurried, deliberate—took longer to resolve out of the darkness than a bright Starfleet uniform should have. Then the light finally settled on a heartbreakingly familiar black-and-violet camouflage, and Chekov's heart sank.

Only to freeze at the base of his throat when he saw the newcomer's face.

He didn't look that different. Chekov thought he

should probably be pleased about that. No gray hair, no dramatic signs of aging in the smooth, clean-shaven face, just a tiredness so profound that Chekov felt almost guilty for succumbing to his own fatigue only a little while ago. His older counterpart didn't even look particularly surprised. He just rubbed at the side of his face almost absently, then turned away from his younger self and focused his attention on Sanner. "Where's Captain Sulu?"

Chekov clenched his teeth on a surge of annoyance. Bad enough to be summarily dismissed by half the senior officers he worked under, he didn't need to tolerate such behavior from himself. "We left him with Mr. Spock, just down the corridor from here." He stopped short of admitting that they didn't know whether or not Captain Sulu was in fact still there. The answer had the virtue of being true without inviting too many uncomfortable questions. He gestured brusquely toward the other column, already fading toward darkness. "As soon as your traveling companion comes through, we'll rejoin them."

The older man stared at him with an expression that might have been mild amusement or disdain. It bothered Chekov a little that he couldn't tell which. How was it possible that he could grow so far away from himself that he couldn't even interpret his own expressions? A flash memory of a Gorn talon sinking into his eye—and he decided he didn't really want to think too much about the answer to that question.

"Ensign Chekov..."

L. A. Graf

Smith's anxious whisper cut across his thoughts, opening a welcome escape route. He turned away from himself, flushing with discomfort, and let Smith distract him with whatever she had to say.

She held out her communicator when he acknowledged her, its antenna grid still open and her face drawn into a frown of worry. "I'm not getting anything from Mr. Spock's party. I've tried calling twice, but nobody answers."

"It's probably the Gate's subspace interference," Sanner suggested, but Smith shook her head.

"I don't think so, sir."

Chekov took the communicator and ran a quick diagnostic, even though nothing seemed amiss on its small display. The open channel hummed faintly, less clear than a good subspace connection ought to be but nothing like the howling static that had characterized their communication attempts when they'd first come into the caves hours before. A query to Spock's communicator produced the expected chirrup of receipt, but no voice followed in response to the call. Chekov folded the communicator shut and bit his lip as he tried to think of what to do.

Like so much else on this ill-fated mission, the Janus Gate made the decision for him.

"Chekov...?"

He turned at the sound of Sulu's voice, a little surprised, but primarily grateful that the Gate had released its last occupant before he was forced to split the party further to investigate the ice cave's silence.

242

Before he'd even finished his turn, though, he saw that the lieutenant's greeting hadn't been meant for him. It was his older self Sulu approached, and his older self who was on the receiving end of the lieutenant's teasing smile.

"Time travel becomes you."

A look of faint embarrassment crossed the older man's face, and he reached up to rub at his cheek again. "A trivial use of medical technology."

The exchange didn't make any sense to Chekov, and he felt strangely excluded from his own life.

Sulu flashed a glance across the rest of the party, looking for someone in particular and obviously not finding them. "Where's Uhura?" he asked worriedly.

That, at least, was something Chekov knew how to answer. "If you'll come with us, sir, we can all find out together."

The conduits had begun to melt.

"This is a good sign!" Sanner enthused as he led them through gathering curtains of pale, clammy mist. "See, the energy storage system for the Gate makes use of an endothermic reaction...."

Chekov didn't bother trying to follow the geologist's explanation, content to relinquish responsibility for the small party to the newly arrived Sulu and...well, to himself. He didn't have to worry anymore about whether going back to the ice cave was the best course of action, or whether wending their way through the dripping, hissing caverns ran too great a risk of someone getting lost. He only had to obey orders, and trust in the wisdom of those whose ranks let them carry more gold on their sleeves. He didn't know whether to feel relieved or disappointed.

Kirk drew up alongside him and watched Sanner paw through the slushing ice ahead of them in search of the latest spot marker. "It's my turn now, isn't it?" he asked Chekov, calmly and quietly. "To go through the device, I mean."

He meant to sound unconcerned, Chekov knew, but instead his voice came out too rigid, too heavy with inappropriate disinterest. Remembering the fear that had been so naked in the boy's face atop the karst plateau, Chekov let the three officers pull a little ahead of them to minimize any chances of being overheard.

"Whether or not they send you will depend on what Mr. Spock decides we have to do about…" He couldn't think of a comfortable way to refer to the man who was also himself, so settled for, "about our extra visitor," as though they were talking about an unexpected guest at a formal dinner. He turned sideways to avoid being doused by the freshly melted water now tumbling out of the hole Captain Kirk had kicked through the ceiling a whole lifetime ago. "We have a few hours left before we have to make any final decisions."

"But you got your pilot back," Kirk pointed out. "You don't have to worry anymore about losing him when the timeline shifts back to where you think it's supposed to be." He shrugged, looking petulant and angry. "That leaves just me to put back where I came from."

Smith splashed a little closer from behind them. "Mr. Spock's getting really good at controlling what the machine does."

Kirk glanced aside at Chekov, then turned his attention pointedly forward, toward the dark figure most plainly visible through the haze of mist ahead of them. "Oh, yeah," he agreed, with deep irony, "I noticed that."

"He can put you back in your timeline a whole day later than you left," Smith persisted, apparently as immune to Kirk's sarcasm as she was to everyone else's. "He can put you in dozens of meters away from where you came out of. We can even send you back with a weapon, so you can defend yourself."

Chekov tried to summarize what he knew Smith meant to convey. "We'll make sure you go back with every advantage we can give you."

Looking down at his feet, Kirk nodded mutely. Chekov knew the games the boy's mind was playing—offering up visions of all the dangers they couldn't possibly predict in advance, all the ways he could die that none of them could help him avoid. He tried to think of something he could say to reassure the boy, but Kirk deflected the effort by asking instead, "Will I remember any of this? Any of you guys, or what happened here?"

Chekov thought about that very seriously. "I don't know," he admitted at last. "Mr. Spock seems to think that once the timeline is repaired and the bubble we constructed collapses, we'll remember our past as a single unbroken timeline, without these changes and interruptions." He hadn't told anyone that he found that thought just a little disturbing. He didn't like the idea of entire days of his life fluttering out of his memory as though they never existed. Even if they never did.

"But what about me?" Kirk asked. Droplets of mist sparkled where they'd gathered on his eyelashes and hair, making him look ephemeral and oddly fragile. "How can I remember my past as one uninterrupted line? I'm here! You guys might be sending me back with a weapon! How am I supposed to not realize that all that happened?"

Chekov didn't know how to answer him except honestly. "I really don't know. I wish I did."

A startled shout from the front of the group clapped off the mist-shrouded walls. Chekov saw the men in front of them stagger to a hurried, uneven halt, then the mist all around came alive with frantic movement. Metal clattered on freshly exposed stone, *snickting* into softened ice to propel intricate black steel bodies up the walls, across the ceiling. Chekov thrust Kirk behind him, felt Smith close in on the other side, and realized almost immediately how pointless the effort had been.

The little metal creatures were everywhere, pressing in from behind, cutting them off from the front. They dropped from the ceiling like fat mechanical spiders, landing with a lightness all out of proportion with their apparent size. They were each one as big as a human head, but with a confusing combination of limbs and what looked like the world's most intricate sensors. One of them scampered forward with its topmost appendages upraised and waving, aiming itself for Kirk, or Chekov, or both.

Smith thrust herself into the thing's path and kicked at it fiercely. Her foot never even made contact. It leaped onto her leg, then away again, too quickly to see precisely what had happened. But the security guard went down as if poleaxed. Chekov tried to catch her, to protect her from cracking her head against the rocks littering the conduit floor. Instead, they went down together in an undignified tangle.

An arm's length away, the swarm of artificial monsters surged back as a group, as though unwilling to make any further contact with the humans. They reformed into a solid, unmoving line, blocking the corridor leading back toward the breakdown exit and the Janus Gate's arrival columns.

Chekov slid himself awkwardly out from under Smith, trying not to let her drop unsupported to the floor. Kirk caught his arm and helped to pull him upright just as someone else took Smith's head in their hands and rolled her neatly to one side to check for a pulse.

"Is she dead?" Kirk asked. He sounded like a boy again, afraid and unsure.

Chekov's older self twitched the faintest hint of a smile. "No. But it stunned her pretty hard." Standing, he hefted her easily over one shoulder and turned to look at Sulu. "I'd suggest we go where they want."

It was only then that Chekov saw the clear path yawning ahead of them. A staccato line of mechanicals decorated the walls leading toward the Janus Gate control room, but they seemed only interested in watching. When Sulu nodded, saying softly, "Stick close," no one breathed so much as an "Aye, sir" in reply. They simply clustered as tightly together as possible and followed him down the silent rows of machines. The little creatures fell in neatly behind them, bringing up the rear like some perverse mechanical guard.

An odd light from the chamber that held the Janus Gate spilled out into the corridor, polluting the mist and staining it a sickly orange. Chekov knew something was wrong even before they rounded the entrance—the earthy smell of melting ice and wet rock had been almost completely overwritten by a harsh, artificial tang, and the sharp clacks and clatters of mechanical industry filled the silence where the Janus Gate's blue force field had hummed only a few short hours ago. The Gate itself had withdrawn back into its silver metal cage, a blue flame heart pulsing to its own alien rhythm.

The entire chamber had been invaded. Elaborate machines, some of them twice the height of a man, surrounded the Janus Gate's central controls or paced the distant perimeter of the cavern. At first, Chekov thought they were only larger versions of the metal creatures who'd surrounded them in the hallway, then one peeled away from the cluster at the control panel and hurried to gather the smaller machines about it like a hen with her chicks. They disappeared into the body of their larger cousin, becoming new convolutions and appendages as though they'd been there all along.

Reassembled, the mother machine all but enveloped Chekov's small party with two of its long arms and pushed them to join their comrades near the middle of the room.

Spock welcomed their arrival with a minute nod of his head, but the humans clustered behind him gave a collective murmur of relief and jostled forward to make contact. Uhura greeted Sulu with a silent hug, and Captain Sulu joined the older Chekov in settling Smith to the ground with no indication of surprise or alarm at seeing him here. Behind them, McCoy coaxed Carolyn Palamas to look up from her hands and see that the others had returned before shouldering his way through the group to kneel beside Chekov next to the unconscious guard.

"What did we miss?" Sanner asked Spock in a low voice.

Spock didn't answer, absorbed in his study of the aliens. They weren't simply robots, Chekov realized. Along the face of each metal torso, a curving length of window revealed a chamber filled with some type of cloudy fluid or gas. A frail, multilegged creature hardly bigger than a skinned dog floated inside, cushioned by some unseen force that kept it steady while still allowing it to flex and turn as its conveyance moved. When one of the complex machines danced up alongside the guards holding them hostage, it moved with a light, incongruous grace, and crouched to a halt much closer than was comfortable with its large size.

"This is the language."

The words, while cool and easily understandable, would never be mistaken for a human's. Even the *Enterprise*'s main computer had more warmth and inflection in its manufactured voice. They extruded from somewhere unidentifiable on the creature's artificial carapace, a lifeless stitchery of sound that might have been individual notes picked out on a toy piano for all the emotion they contained. It had no recognizable face and precious little movement in its limbs, so it was impossible to tell if it meant the words as a statement or a question.

Spock cocked his head as though he found the attempt at communication fascinating. "Yes, that is the language we understand."

A complex series of movements, too fast and delicate for the eye to follow, produced what Chekov recognized as Uhura's archaeological translator. The alien offered it on the end of one extended appendage. After a moment, Spock reached up to take it, then passed it behind him to Uhura without turning around.

Without warning, the creature whirled away and scuttled back to rejoin its brethren at the Janus Gate console. Blue light glowed warmly on the face of its transparent tank. "This is the language," it announced again in its flat alien voice. "We are Shechenag." As a single gesture, each of the aliens surrounding the Janus Gate pattered complicated hands over the surface of the machine. Looking for something. Reassuring themselves. "This device falls outside your jurisdiction. You will leave now."

A wave of alarm swept through the small group. McCoy started to protest, but Chekov shushed him with a hand on his arm.

"It is not our intention to trespass," Spock said calmly, as though reasoning with grotesquely inhuman aliens were part of his everyday duties. "However, this device has displaced one of our companions—"

"This is understood." An almost panicked spasm of movement flashed among the aliens, then stilled again. "Damage to the timescape cannot be undone through further damage. This device causes damage. This device must not be active."

Something that might have been irritation knit together on Spock's brow, but nothing in his voice or stance betrayed any emotion. "Are you the original architects of this device?"

"We are Shechenag. This device must not be active." The mother hen device hurried toward them again, arms outflung and quivering. The sharp *snick* of metal slashing against metal could only be a threat, no matter how placid the voice of the creature speaking. "You must take your vessel now and leave this space. We give you ten hours to do so."

TO BE CONTINUED
in
BOOK THREE: *PAST PROLOGUE*

Look for STAR TREK fiction from Pocket Books

Star Trek®

Star Trek: The Next Generation®

Enterprise™

Star Trek®: New Frontier

Star Trek®: Stargazer

The Valiant • Michael Jan Friedman
Double Helix #6: The First Virtue • Michael Jan Friedman and Christie
    Golden
Gauntlet • Michael Jan Friedman
Progenitor • Michael Jan Friedman

Star Trek®: Starfleet Corps of Engineers (eBooks)

Have Tech, Will Travel (paperback) • various
  #1 • *The Belly of the Beast* • Dean Wesley Smith
  #2 • *Fatal Error* • Keith R.A. DeCandido
  #3 • *Hard Crash* • Christie Golden
  #4 • *Interphase, Book One* • Dayton Ward & Kevin Dilmore
Miracle Workers (paperback) • various
  #5 • *Interphase, Book Two* • Dayton Ward & Kevin Dilmore
  #6 • *Cold Fusion* • Keith R.A. DeCandido
  #7 • *Invincible, Book One* • Keith R.A. DeCandido & David Mack
  #8 • *Invincible, Book Two* • Keith R.A. DeCandido & David Mack
  #9 • *The Riddled Post* • Aaron Rosenberg
  #10 • *Gateways Epilogue: Here There Be Monsters* • Keith R.A. DeCandido
  #11 • *Ambush* • Dave Galanter & Greg Brodeur
  #12 • *Some Assembly Required* • Scott Ciencin & Dan Jolley
  #13 • *No Surrender* • Jeff Mariotte
  #14 • *Caveat Emptor* • Ian Edginton
  #15 • *Past Life* • Robert Greenberger
  #16 • *Oaths* • Glenn Hauman

Star Trek®: Invasion!

#1 • *First Strike* • Diane Carey
#2 • *The Soldiers of Fear* • Dean Wesley Smith & Kristine Kathryn Rusch
#3 • *Time's Enemy* • L.A. Graf
#4 • *The Final Fury* • Dafydd ab Hugh
Invasion! Omnibus • various

Star Trek®: Day of Honor

#1 • *Ancient Blood* • Diane Carey
#2 • *Armageddon Sky* • L.A. Graf
#3 • *Her Klingon Soul* • Michael Jan Friedman
#4 • *Treaty's Law* • Dean Wesley Smith & Kristine Kathryn Rusch
The Television Episode • Michael Jan Friedman
Day of Honor Omnibus • various

Star Trek®: The Captain's Table

#1 • *War Dragons* • L.A. Graf
#2 • *Dujonian's Hoard* • Michael Jan Friedman
#3 • *The Mist* • Dean Wesley Smith & Kristine Kathryn Rusch
#4 • *Fire Ship* • Diane Carey
#5 • *Once Burned* • Peter David
#6 • *Where Sea Meets Sky* • Jerry Oltion
The Captain's Table Omnibus • various

Star Trek®: The Dominion War

#1 • *Behind Enemy Lines* • John Vornholt
#2 • *Call to Arms...* • Diane Carey
#3 • *Tunnel Through the Stars* • John Vornholt
#4 • *...Sacrifice of Angels* • Diane Carey

Star Trek®: Section 31™

Rogue • Andy Mangels & Michael A. Martin
Shadow • Dean Wesley Smith & Kristine Kathryn Rusch
Cloak • S. D. Perry
Abyss • Dean Weddle & Jeffrey Lang

Star Trek®: Gateways

#1 • *One Small Step* • Susan Wright
#2 • *Chainmail* • Diane Carey
#3 • *Doors Into Chaos* • Robert Greenberger
#4 • *Demons of Air and Darkness* • Keith R.A. DeCandido
#5 • *No Man's Land* • Christie Golden
#6 • *Cold Wars* • Peter David
#7 • *What Lay Beyond* • various

Star Trek®: The Badlands

#1 • Susan Wright
#2 • Susan Wright

Star Trek®: Dark Passions

#1 • Susan Wright
#2 • Susan Wright

Star Trek® Omnibus Editions

Invasion! Omnibus • various
Day of Honor Omnibus • various

The Captain's Table Omnibus • various
Star Trek: Odyssey • William Shatner with Judith and Garfield Reeves-Stevens
Millennium Omnibus • Judith and Garfield Reeves-Stevens
Starfleet: Year One • Michael Jan Friedman

Other Star Trek® Fiction

Legends of the Ferengi • Ira Steven Behr & Robert Hewitt Wolfe
Strange New Worlds, vol. I, II, III, IV, and V • Dean Wesley Smith, ed.
Adventures in Time and Space • Mary P. Taylor, ed.
Captain Proton: Defender of the Earth • D.W. "Prof" Smith
New Worlds, New Civilizations • Michael Jan Friedman
The Lives of Dax • Marco Palmieri, ed.
The Klingon Hamlet • Wil'yam Shex'pir
Enterprise Logs • Carol Greenburg, ed.